THE NEXT MOTHER

The Next Mother

Stories

Jack Donahue

BROKEN TRIBE PRESS

CONTENTS

ENLIGHTMENT AT BIG BEND

Most people wouldn't recognize truth if a cow came along and plopped it on their face. My advice is follow your heart. Don't worry about the truth so much. Most times it's just like a little fly buzzing around a cow's ass. You can't catch it. You just kinda swat at it. Whereas in Texas, you can be as imprecise as you wish. Just do it in a grand way. Do it the Texas way! I mean, you should try to do things well, but if that fails, just do 'em big. You gotta come on with blaring horns and eyes wide open. Be confident, even if you're ignorant. Because the world will say, there is someone who made some noise. There is someone who made his mark. I'm telling you, you might never be famous in Texas, because of all the greats who've come before you, but if you're loud enough, you'll always be heard. It'll be my pleasure to show you how to do it ... the Texas way.

I'm talking about me of course, the big Texas tycoon, owner of King Rex cattle ranch. More head of cattle than the population of some major cities and more acreage than several states. But my prosperity is just an accident of my circumstances or should I say the adversity of my birth was reversed and this is what I wound up with. Let me back up a bit. I gotta tell you a little about my upbringing but I won't dwell on the subject. I promise.

My mother got sick right after I was born and she died just seven days later so I never got to suckle her breast. I can't say that I rightly remember her but I sure do miss what she was supposed to be - a nurturing, loving mother of the earth. My dad said he did the best he could to raise me but he didn't know nothing about mothering and he actually did a pretty lousy job of fathering as well. But I was a real independent sort, never had too much use for school which I skipped a lot. Dad would get all sorts of pissed off when he had to leave work as a railroad superintendent and listen to some old hag of a teacher tell him what a miscreant truant I was.

Then, he met some young bitch who sure was pretty but sure wasn't the mothering type, at least to a twelve year old boy like myself. She gave me the kind of look that said look out boy, I got your father by his kaks and I ain't letting go. That's when I went. I just put on my sneakers and jeans and flannel shirt, rolled up a big wool blanket inside a rubber mat, into which I also inserted my trusty pocket knife, stole some money out of my old man's drawer where he kept his cash, condoms and cufflinks, left the house for good and never looked back. And I've been a miscreant truant ever since.

Folks call me Great River by the way. I'm great all right. Big and fat and larger than life. Anyhow, the spirit moved me when I was young to go on this odyssey ... Texas style. Some voice inside me told me to hike the entirety of the Rio Grande river, the Texas part of it anyway. I mean, come on, when you think Rio Grande, you think Texas, right? Well, so do I. Who cares if it trickles through Colorado and New Mexico? The Mexicans make an unsubstantiated claim to that river too. But I can refute that. Hell, they don't even call it Rio Grande. To them, it's Rio Bravo del Norte or some crap like that. I'll get to that subject later. Right now, what's important is that you understand that the Rio Grande is Texas and Texas is the Rio Grande, okay? Sure I was a little scared at first. It was just me and the river, me and the desert, me and the mountains, me and the sky.

I started my journey just north of the city line at El Paso, right where it meets the New Mexico border on Mesa Boulevard. As far as I was concerned, this was the source of the mighty Rio Grande, yet not so mighty at that point … a low and slow flat-water … kind of meanders around rocks and mud bars, brown and sluggish, moving absentmindedly along its marshy path of tree-lined banks …quiet, serene… the fastest things moving were the fluttering humming bird's wings as he sucked the flowers on the ocotillo bush. Later on when it reached very rugged and very unsettled land, the river became wild, bold, turbulent and restless but I don't want to get ahead of myself. Anyhow, my intention was to walk and swim, to navigate that river from one end to the other. I did that for a year. I guess it took that long. I never did see a newspaper, hear a radio or watch a TV show. Sometimes I'd get news from stray campers and sometimes when they weren't looking I'd steal some of their equipment. But I was only a boy and I had to survive. I can still hear some of them yelling at me as I shot the whitewater rapids the hell out of there in their brand new canoe. I was a hundred yards downriver before they knew what hit them. Once I met a Chisos Indian in the desert who tried to teach me the language of the earth, *terra lingua* I think he called it. And he'd say things like the ground shake, the cloud rinse, the rain dance, and the animals eat one another but I told him I wanted to learn the language of the river, *rio lingua*, and he'd say the river flow, flow and flow.

The river formed me like no mother or father or state institution ever could. When you're as young as I was, what do you know? What you don't know is your limitations. All I had were the looming mountains, stark desert landscapes, and a glistening ribbon of water slicing through it all. It was just me riding its currents. I had no ceiling but the open sky. I never worried that my father got frantic and came looking for me. He had that younger woman he could cozy up to each night and I'm sure she had all his railroad stock and whatever the hell else she wanted. They had each other and they didn't have me. I had the river. You can see from my wide girth that I didn't exactly starve to death. The river, mountains and desert were plentiful. I knew what was happening to me as it happened. The river cured me of any troublesome thought I might've had. Thinking wouldn't convince me one way or the other whether my father was dead or alive and if he was alive, that he was looking for me. The river washed all that away, cleansed me of the past so that only the present and the near future mattered. Yessir, the river made a man of me at twelve and thirteen years of age. I said goodbye to boyhood and went forever forward from that day.

Life just poured out of me. It's here in my heart and I just let it live itself out. Now, when I am with people, I know their hearts and I know their minds. The river gave that to me. It's a gift. I accepted it graciously. I cannot let people know that I know them, that I can see inside. If I do, they will become something else. And, where would that get any of us? My enlightenment came at a bend in the river, at the Big Bend. I didn't even know where I was until years later I consulted a map and saw how the southern flowing river took a northerly course.

But before my big enlightenment I had several little ones, thinking along the way that this was it, that I knew all I had to know. One day I crawled out of the riverbed, on to a rock plateau, exhausted from my journey. I lie down next to a small tide pool. I fell asleep in the hot afternoon sun and when I awoke, the pool had evaporated to just a tiny puddle and there lying next to me is this creature. I did not know what it was, half-dead, limp, struggling for existence. It had a long, slippery body of a snake and the head of a lizard-to-be, with little rib-like slits on its belly, as if it wanted to have legs, but was afraid to break through. The creature couldn't decide if it needed dryness or wetness. It was half in the puddle and half out. So I grabbed it, stroked it and ultimately gave it life. I lost myself in that hour. I no longer felt the need to prove anything to myself and I thought my journey ended right there on that rock. Did I need to go further? Did I have to reach the river's end? I thought I found what I was looking for even though I didn't know what I was looking for.

But then the river laughed at me and the canyons echoed go further. I knew the river has many goals: the waterfalls; the ripping current; the charge to the sea; the vapor and rise; be the recipient of heavy rains. My bare feet danced on the shimmering oven-hot limestone flats and prickly burrs stuck to the back of my calves with each step I took. Ribbons of colors waved snake-like before me as I followed the river around the next bend. I ran out of bank and had to jump in the river. It flow hard and wild. It don't mean no harm but if harm got in its way, the river run right over it and push it out of the way always changing, always going somewhere. It pushed me down about three hundred yards, twisting and turning my skinny thirteen-year-old body. I had no choice but to just go with it, no will of my own, no match for this wild water. I grabbed reeds and the river pulled me and the reeds. I landed on a sandy beach, beneath a big palm. Exhausted, I collapsed, scarred and beaten.

I awoke just before sunrise and walked along the river in the ambient light of the starry night. I noticed that I walked with two shadows of myself, one behind me and one before me, identical twin silhouettes of my very self, mimicking my every move. I moved within a timeless continuum, in which the past and the future mirrored themselves and my self. I thought I must be imagining all of this, or that someone was following me, but I positioned my head in such a way that one eye could look behind while the other eye looked ahead and my two shadows were as real and consistent as my breathing. Then, I walked some more in the company of my shadows, understanding the *terra lingua* my Indian friend told me about, and the *rio lingua,* the *cielo lingua.*

In one moment, as I slowed down, not knowing that I was coming nearer to my ultimate destination, I observed a third shadow, directly on my left side. And, it was in that moment when the past, the present, and the future converged into one being and then all three disappeared as quickly as they came. In that instant, that timeless moment, I understood the reason for my existence. I am the river. I am the desert. I am the mountains. But is there more? Am I something else? What is missing? That night I lay under the stars of the new moon and it was as if a diamond merchant locked me in the darkest room and said I will now present to you the world's most precious gems. I was completely enclosed within the heavens, every constellation, every planet, every star, every moon and heavenly comet made their majestic appearance before my eyes. Yep, the Milky Way and all his friends were out that night. And the Lone Star of Texas shone the brightest among the bright. And don't tell me, that these same stars spilled over into the Mexican sky. Oh no, this was a Texas phenomenon. It was almost too much beauty to absorb in one night.

But that was nothing compared to what was to come. I hardly slept but was not tired as I continued my descent down the river, through the majestic canyons and around the blind bends. The river was low and I saw mule deer tracks, followed by mountain lion tracks and found the spot where the dry earth was severely disturbed where the predator dragged its prey into the woods and as my Chisos friend said one animal did eat another.

Then, in a moment, in the mystery and apparition of the towering Santa Elena canyon I came to my journey's end on a grassy vega. The stone walls were sixteen hundred feet high and there she stood but five and one half feet high. The limbs of cottonwoods and willows framed her red dress, black hair and light brown skin against a bright blue sky. She beckoned me forward. She knelt down and picked the prickly burrs out of my feet and washed the blood off in the muddy river, now quiet and subdued. She rested my wounded foot in the fold of her dress between her legs. My foot, then my whole body felt the warmth of her womb and I knew that this was the place, the source of motherhood and the gateway to sexual pleasure. She then rested my foot gently on the hot limestone flat and rose to her full height. She bent over, crisscrossed her arms and lifted her dress straight over her head. This unveiling seemed to take place in slow motion in one fluid, rapturous movement. Even though I didn't know the exact word for it then, I said something like thank you God for making me sexual. She then helped me remove my clothes and our naked bodies touched and she taught me all the sensitive parts of my own body, then hers. She was a Mexican princess with Indian features and her timeless beauty would make the most confident Conquistador stumble over his words and tremble in his boots. She took me into her secret chamber and I wanted to marry her but she did not take my seed but let the river have it. You're married to the river now, she told me. But I longed for her and tried to swim back, but even though the river was mild and timid in this canyon hollow, with hardly a ripple, it would not let me go back. It would only take me forever forward.

So my seed flowed with the grit and stone, and continued to cut a deeper and wider canyon along the river's path. Needless to say, even to this day, I have never met a more beautiful woman and she wasn't even a Texan. There was discovery around each bend in the river. Every one. I know. I discovered them for myself. But I did not travel the river for its entire length as was my original plan. I ended my journey just beyond the big bend. That is where I became enlightened which would set the course for the rest of my life. So, that's my story of the river in all its primitive beauty, its inexorable flow to the sea, its constant renewal from the skies, its indiscriminate ripping apart of canyon walls, its reforming nature, its desire only for itself, its knowledge that it is more powerful than anything around it or in it. I left the river and travelled by foot along the shimmering flats of the Chihuahua desert and ascended the rim rocks of the great mountains. I hiked through the Rio Grande floodplains to arid badlands to sotol grasslands to rugged volcanic peaks. I did not head home. I no longer had a home. Only the present hour and the future day, beneath the stars of an unknown god. The river took me in and taught me what I needed to know. I am the desert. I am the sky and the stars. I am the mountains. I am the river. I AM TEXAS!

Y'all have heard that cliché that life is a journey. Well, it sure is. Many years after I made that journey as an adolescent along the Rio Grande, I revisited the scene of my enlightenment. Like they say, there's no going home again. Instead of a beautiful, young Mexican princess willing to introduce me to the pleasures of sexual bliss I met an old, wrinkled Mexican beggar woman, looking like one of those stones that had fallen from the edge of the Santa Elena canyon – body broken to pieces, skin punished by the sun with gray, straw hair matted and unclean. She was begging for coins and trying to sell some handmade silver jewelry that I had no interest in and no one to give them to. It did surprise me though that I realized I had survived this hostile environment as a young man. I must have been like one of those weeds that keeps popping up in the cracks of a sidewalk. They can grow anywhere. I grew up there, like the chuquilla and candelilla in the arid limestone flats of the Chihuahua desert. These plants shoot down shallow roots and leave the soil rough and strong with only a few deep pockets to hold water and nutrients.

The second time around wasn't a wilderness trip for me. I stayed in the National Park Service barracks at Big Bend, primitive by Triple A standards. After all, I had to make my own bed if I was so inclined, but my room had air conditioning. No phone. No TV. But it was free of bugs. Every night, just around dusk I walked out on the narrow porch and looked over the ledge to observe my friend, Pepe Le P-U, who arrived at the same spot at the same time every night.

Actually, if his reputation didn't precede him, you'd a thought he was a beautiful creature, a large alpha male skunk with a broad white stripe stretching from the top of his small head to the tip of his broad, bushy tail. I never did know if he was aware of the fact that I was staring at him, admiring him for all the time he was in my sight. I imagine that he was fully aware of my presence but I posed no threat to him nor was I of any keen interest to him as he was to me. Every single night he came up to the barracks and pissed on the south wall. I don't know if he was marking his territory or what but I realized that this amazing critter was at the very top of his own food chain. He wasn't on anyone else's menu. There wasn't a mountain lion or black bear that would even consider messing with him. I could take my clothes off and jump into a tomato juice bath for a week if he ever took aim at me but the furry creatures of the forest would have to live with his stink for a long time and they knew it. They had no interest in stinking for stink's sake. So little Pepe Le P-U strolled about with the greatest confidence in the world. I'm sure he had some concerns but I didn't notice any. And I thought, why this vile little vessel of unending stink bombs has found peace in this crazy world: confident, unafraid of anything larger or smaller than himself. It's like his search for the universal truth in nature, if he was given to searching, was actually contained within his own being, kind of like a built-in, self-contained nirvana. What he was and where he was going were the same thing. It occurred to me, philosophically that is, there are certain beings you need to just leave alone, walk away from, so to speak, because you can never win a pissing contest with a skunk.

After one's big enlightenment, it's either time to die, a time to move on, or a time to experience other, smaller enlightenments. So, before I left the Big Bend this second time around, I went a little further along the Lost Mine Trail that I abandoned when I was just a skinny, little kid. Sure enough, it again led to nowhere. But it made me wonder: how many skeletons are sitting around on the ground somewhere, some with their hats still on, sinking further into oblivion, deep in the bowels of the earth while the rest of us are left on top trying to make sense out of this world. This is our time and we got to make the most of it, I guess.

Before I head home, I think I'll visit the river again. That's what I'm going to do. I'll finish hiking that desert and mountain and finish my journey in the river. The Great River. The Rio Grande. I'll get myself in shape like I was when I was a wiry thirteen-year-old, full of piss and vinegar with a lust for life as big and grand as the river itself. That's what I'm gonna do. The river is where I need to go. I'll return to my own Garden of Eden. Shalom. The river is revelation. That's what is. The river is revelation.

ASYLUM, ASYLUM

My name is Oliver Seawagon. I don't create music. I coax it. Out of the wind. Out of the sea. Out of the earth. I harness the elements, gather nature's whole, half and quarter notes, monitor pitch and frequency, capture the lowing and mewing tones of the tides, so that the music of the wind, sea, and earth soothes the savage refugees before they drown.

Having no choice but to witness the life and death struggle of desperate refugees changed my life, not necessarily for the better. Yet, it made me think of actually doing something for them. It forced me to be realistic about my options. I can't save them. I don't own a boat, am classified as a weak swimmer and I live in a tiny cabin, no bigger than a tool shed. What can I do to ease their pain?

Noah built an ark. I will build a harp!

Week after week I walk to the edge of the cliff and see men, women and children in a broken down boat with not enough room to sit or kneel, massed together in the smell and discomfort of a vessel with a maximum capacity one tenth their number. God knows how many days they have been at sea. I fix my mind on building them a giant harp that will calm them while they await the heliocopters and rescue boats. It would give me a fair amount of pleasure to watch the swimmers from the overturned boats cock their heads to listen and try to see where the strange, otherworldly sounds are coming from. It will be a sweet beckoning call as they would realize, in one delusional but hopeful moment, that the shore is within reach, whether friendly or otherwise.

I live on the rocky west coast of an island, on a promontory, with a delicious view of the cruel, unforgiving sea. If you've ever been to Ireland, my dot of island real estate is somewhat like the Cliffs of Moher, without the tourists. My home, however, is much further downstream from the welcoming green and aromatic burning peat of mother Ireland. It is nearer the ports of rejection and the harbors of futile attempts at a better, safer life. Although I long ago abandoned any access to electronic and print media, all the signs below me point to a refugee crisis. This poses a real threat to my reclusive, peaceful existence. I'm no humanitarian but I feel compelled to respond to the crisis in some way.

For the last ten years or so, I have managed to avoid contact with others of my species, even postal workers. When I moved, I failed to notify anyone of my forwarding address. It's not that I dislike people, with the exception of a handful of uninspiring types who exercised authority over me for short bursts of time, grilling me, questioning my art even before projects were even finished, each one of them having ingested mega doses of the stupid pill just before making my life miserable. Their only contribution was to pay for my projects. They could do little else. A grimy handful of these people also managed to distort my sense of inner peace. Their pernicious haranguing provided the foundation for my troubling thoughts. I'm not especially proud of what occupies my mind but it has a persistent amount of staying power.

At various times, I envision strapping one of these perpetrators into a supermarket shopping cart like a bratty two-year old, then steer the carriage on a thrilling downhill slope leading to the cliff's edge. Then, as I am incapable of controlling my malignant thoughts, kick the cart a little nudge with my foot, launching it off the edge of a cliff, much like the one I live on right now. For the meaner individuals, the really airtight sphincter types, I dream up longer, more prolonged miseries. For example, much like a recurring nightmare, I say to them may all your daughters grow up to be the village whores you bilious, self-righteous, blood vitiated ass pimples. You taught her all the right things, so you think, and she hooks up with some druggie chug-a-lug excuse for a human being, many stops beneath her station. The sleek express train passes her by, and she winds up with the never on time local. For several years she'll torment you with too much news of her dissolute life showered with constant, plaintive requests for cash, you know for essential things like potato chips, condoms and beer, then she'll dump him and do you a big favor by returning home to finish her doctoral thesis "The Habits of Sea Microbes as They Crawl up the Asses of Land Animals". Make no mistake. She will convince you it is an important work of biological scholarship. Mostly because she's still your little girl, you believe every word she says. Privately, you decide to never again sit on a sandy beach.

Actually, there are some people I have liked in the past but I'm not sure they ever for a moment liked me in return. I'm much better off without the grant givers and paperwork pensioners. Less toxic bile in my gut. Once I retired and secured this parcel of extreme waterfront property, I built my own cabin. Not much of a nature boy but stubborn enough to live off the land and the sea. Some years ago, I made earth music, or wind music, to sustain myself and fulfill my grandiose creative urges. Big installations, in major cities all over the world. Something like Christo and Jeanne-Claude, but without the umbrellas, sheets and barrels. I use wires, long steel wires, strung out over boulevards or from tall buildings to a fixed point on the street, like gigantic Aeolian harps, heavenly angel strings as some people liked to call them. Hundreds, sometimes thousands of people would show up for a performance, and listen to this most public of music. Most preferred the music emanating from my installation over that being proffered at the free summer concerts in the parks, not having to drag lawn chairs and greasy KFC chicken buckets to listen to some bent-over, farty old banjo players dressed in boaters and wide, red suspenders. sporting smug, toothy smiles, honorifically commissioned to sit in the town square gazebo and cheerfully pluck out eminently forgettable tunes for the lawn squatters.

Some of those attending my installations, elitists some might characterize them as such, would confide in me afterwards that even though my instrument was massive, they experienced a sense of intimacy with the music that they seldom found within a velvet-draped concert hall at five hundred dollars a seat.

Here's how it worked during my professional career. Once the crew and I rigged everything up over the course of several weeks, I would gently grasp the wires, give them an encouraging tug, then let the wind and the vagaries of strung steel do the rest. Music is never for the masses. It is always for an audience of one. You, for instance. You, in particular. Just you. That's my theory.

Granted, my current state of mind is not especially healthy. It is difficult for me to employ the word 'living' in terms of what I provided for music lovers around the world for so many years, since I consider myself an artist. Yet what I did I got paid for. I've learned to avoid looking back on past mistakes. That futile exercise might negate everything I've done up until this point in my life. Whether or not I ever had a burning passion for my art or just fell into the world of natural music is immaterial at this juncture. Most people throughout history just did the next best thing that came along and called it a career, or a vocation, or a calling. The ones who identified whatever they did as a passion usually never had to pay the utility bill. Putting aside all the shards of broken relationships in my life (actually they weren't broken as much as they didn't exist in that I made every attempt to avoid encountering anyone with conflict programmed into their psyche) some might judge my situation to contain the essence of an unfulfilled life. Get a load of me. Confessing the possibility of failure.

Aside from these unsolicited opinions, I did manage to create beauty in this world. And maybe there are some people out there who made real life connections with others *because* of my efforts. I once got invited to participate in a public forum following a major installation, to discuss my art and engage with the audience but that didn't last long. I couldn't stand one more dumb, ignorant question and walked out. I sensed a hostile environment. Never again I told myself. Hemingway said something like it's only people who could ruin a day and for that bit of sophistry, I proclaim him a prophet. Anyway, getting back to my primary occupation, or preoccupation or just let me call it art, I want to tell you about the wind harp.

It may look elaborate but a wind harp is a simple instrument. Even a light wind will cause it to make music. My basic design uses eight steel strings with magnetic pickups made with nails. For this, my final project, I mounted the wind harp from the top of a shed and drew the wires down to the rocks, some of them submerged in water at high tide. I used 1/2 inch steel angles at the ends to support the wires in the rocks with screw eyebolts. Previously, I experimented with different thicknesses for different sounds but long ago settled on 24-gauge solid steel wire for the strings. The strings' vibrations interact with the magnetic field produced by the pickup coils. The wind blows above, below and across the strings, causing natural vibrations at various harmonies of the strings' fundamental frequency. If you pluck the string, the sound of this fundamental frequency will be heard. As the wind itself is always unpredictable, it comes as no surprise that it causes multiples of that frequency to vibrate up and down the entire length of the wire. For the most ideal harmony, I systematically loosen or tighten the tension on the eyebolts so all the wires perform at the same frequency. The inner wires make the most significant musical sounds, while the outer passive wires add complimentary sound through the connection at the single eyebolt end. Higher winds naturally create higher frequencies. When it rains, the wind harp now becomes a glorious rain harp, making very pleasant tones as raindrops hit the wires. Just think of how pleasant and peaceful your experience is when you listen to raindrops land on a thin metal surface, or to listen closely to the syrupy drops falling from an oar into the water as it is lifted in and out of a tranquil pond. Now imagine the rain, wind and the movement within the massive sea boulders coalescing into an unpredictable set, then another, each quite different than the previous one.

Before I quit the worldwide installation circuit, I hoarded as much steel wire as I could and spent my last dollar transporting the massive coils and necessary tools to where I now live. Okay, I borrowed a few pieces here and there. Like taking home staplers, paper clips, pens and notepads from a clerical job. Everyone does it. Try not to judge me.

I never thought I'd continue making giant installations but secured the tools and materials just in case. I always wanted to build a wind harp simply for my own pleasure without the benefit of a government grant or with the help of a competent tech crew. Just with my two grimy hands and my own bullheaded grit set free to make mistakes no one would ever know about. I deliberately made the last harp simple, crude even, without any recognizable border simulating a real factory-made harp. Closer to nature, I thought.

It didn't look like the fleet of refugees would end their overly ambitious journeys to freedom and safety any time soon. I wanted this harp to be anonymous, unseen, installed at a point where sea meets land in order to provide a soothing listening experience for the refugees as they struggle to reach the shore. One could hardly see the wires from a distance, especially since I designed the instrument so it would blend into the environs. A strong gleam of sunshine would just make it look like the sun was playing its usual tricks with the rocks, earth, sea and sky.

This endeavor would be more fulfilling than anything I ever did for money. I had a good run when I built harps professionally but had to give it up as my bank account dwindled close to zero. Pensions don't exist for independent builders of wind harps. I just made sure I put enough cash aside to get out of town and live the simple life. An artist can't survive on government commissions. I needed to put some years between my aesthetic judgment concerning art and my feelings of guilt for creating art that depended on the largesse of others, most pointedly the stiff-necked bureaucrats who populate this planet in abundance. To do it simply for pleasure was something I seldom experienced when I was so intensely proprietary about my art. Why hadn't I acted on this earlier? The real life drama of the refugee crisis, arriving at my doorstep so to speak, inspired me. Once the decision was made, I immediately felt like I started to breathe unpolluted air. Strangely, I got this urge to live fully while observing other people dying.

The scene was all too familiar and unsettling. There, below me, bobbing up and down on the rough sea like so many discarded plastic containers, clothed in useless makeshift life jackets, desperately trying to hold on to the last thin thread of life, clinging as best they could to pieces of the doomed craft they sailed their bodies and hopes on, along with other unfortunate souls grabbing on to the floating body nearest them, whether dead or alive. It is more than a fair bet that the bloated bodies were their life rafts in the guise of a most recently deceased mother, or aunt, or brother, son or daughter. Their plan, designed under fire or in the stare of a machete, was to keep the family together. Still others, independent, stronger swimmers capable of resisting the waves a minute or two longer, flapped about, draining whatever energy was left in their spent bodies, crying out in languages I did not understand.

The sea is never consistent, except in the category of forgiveness. It chooses to forget but never forgive. Here, water never laps on the shore in some fiction of a romantic, moonlit night. It pounds the shore. It crashes the rocks. Each wave carries a load of bodies bound in their Promethean chains, lifting them higher with each violent thrust, forcing their fragile human flesh to meet the jagged, immovable tombstone rocks. If the sea didn't kill them, the rocks certainly would. I remembered one childhood Bible lesson and hoped that I will not be the one blessed who seizes the Babylonian babies and dashes them upon the rocks. This thought came to mind as I began to understand that the music flowing from the harp I built, rather than giving them a peaceful transition to the next world, violated their spirits and pounded their souls into submission as much as the sea and the rocks tore their bodies to shreds.

On this day of screaming in your dreams horror, I recognized my fatal error, made possible only by a lifelong aversion to the care and nurturing of others. I forced myself to look but covered my ears to muffle the hopeless screeches and screams, the grotesque, ungodly vocal articulations of their death throes that harmonized eerily with the wind harp I built to offer just the opposite of what they are now forced to endure. Now the music was entirely oppositional, functioning madly in a twisted and hideous turn of fortune, sadistically doing further damage to the savage refugees before they drowned in this foreign, adversarial sea.

On this day, the same soul-piercing wind and wild currents that overturned the boat, pitched a sinister tone to the wind harp. It's not like you can simply plug in your favorite tune appropriate for the moment. The unpredictable movements of the wind and sea dictate every selection. The music I allowed, or forced them to hear, was otherworldly, ghostly, like a long, whipsaw slash into the flesh of the soul. Not a superficial flesh wound. They already had enough of those, but a deep soul wound. It was bloody, savage, and damningly eternal. It reverberated in their ears in a shocking, fearsome discordant crescendo of a force out of control coming right at them, uncaring in its haphazard path of destruction, rendering the swimmers utterly helpless, like being tied to a tree in the midst of a tornado's vortex. I witnessed this as just as hardened and ingrained as the music I delivered to these lost souls, sliming out of capsized boats like half-dead worms escaping a bait box.

This wind, sea and earth music came not from a loving but an angry God. It prefigured hell for them, this music, the kind of hell that is truly unending. Swimming for all eternity in the devil's vile broth. This is not a peaceful passing in the loving whisper of death. The brain and the heart were sliced open in the unanesthesized root canal of consciousness.

Not long afterwards, heliocopters flew overhead. Rescue boats came to collect the bodies. There is no soft landing on this rocky coast. It is not a place any person with even a minimal knowledge of the sea would navigate to. Other peoples in other lands must have turned them away by policy and decree, safely distant from the horrific result of their decision-making process.

Hours after the last rescue boat motored away, when all the dead bodies were placed in bags and the half dead were hoisted into the boats, with little daylight left to this gloom-ridden day, I saw what looked like a small animal or child bobbing on the surface of the still stormy sea. The violent wind music even more persistent and penetrating than before. I grabbed my wire cutter and ran down to the rocks. The sea pushed the flailing object closer, to within twenty yards. I could tell it was a child, a small, weakened boy with such little life left, clinging to what looked like a moss laden log. Then, the log flipped over and the tree had a face, eyes, nose, hair and water pouring in and out of a dead mouth like the very last spurts of a garden hose when the spigot is shut. Then, I could see the ugly truth that boy held on to the shredded blouse of a dead woman. My spirit spoke. Save the boy.

I cut the wires. In one violent, danger filled instant, the tense strands of steel kicked out like a feral beast released from its cage, making a demonic whipping sound as they hurtled skyward, following a wild, zigzag path, slicing through several seagulls flying overhead, cutting them to pieces in a furious flurry of feathers, blood and guts. Now I must swim against the current.

The boy is dark skinned. Maybe Arab or Indian. His hair is black and curly. His eyes, big, vacant, with long lashes blinking as if to signal me. If he had any tears to shed, the perpetual flood of waves washed them away. His lips were swollen. The waves push him even closer, close enough that I could see he was wearing a bright orange T-shirt with two identical words stitched one on top of the other in letters cut from a thick black fabric. The two words screamed at me through the wash of the foamy sea: *Asylum, Asylum.*

I try to swim to him. I duck under each wave rather than fight them. Now he is separated from the body he clung to. Was that his mother? Is she the one who sewed *Asylum, Asylum* on his shirt? What is going through his mind, seeing, in his abridged edition of a life, a mother who pushed him forth from her womb, sustaining him with milk flowing from her breasts, now lastly functioning as a floating dock without a permit from the town board.

I must save him. She became his homemade, buoyant life jacket. It is now my turn. The first terrifying moment he stepped into that boat, his boyhood was stolen from him. What kind of hand has been dealt to him, barely five or six years old? Will he get a chance to play it? Can he see me coming toward him?

I must save him. He drifts further away as my mind drifts in the solemn rhythm of the sea. I am beyond weary. My mind commands my arms to move but they are deadened by the powerful sea. I am limp. Useless. I see the boy's face again. It reminds me of my father's face, the last time I ever saw him. I was around this boy's age. The doorbell rang but mother told me not to answer it. I looked through the peephole and beheld the lasting image of a broken man, my father, drunk, spilled out on the hallway floor, a vacant look about his eyes that said I just want to come home. I'm the only one left who can save this boy, give him a warm home, food and clothing. The whirlpool is spinning me like a cruel, cosmic joke. His lips barely move but they mouth the words *Asylum, Asylum.* I sink and bob back up. I am drifting. He's getting away from me. Maybe teach him how to whittle wood, start a fire, what plants are safe to eat, how to survive – no, he is a survivor already. How to *live* as a boy. All the things a kid should do - Funland - arcade - coins galore, I'll be his ATM, just keep feeding him game tokens - No swimming. No water parks!

First a doctor to check him out head to toe, inside and out, put him in school, find a mother somewhere. I hear more admonitions of that same psalm: there we sat down and there we wept. On the willows there we hung up our harps. I swear on my father's grave I'll never again build another harp. I must save him. He is not a savage. He is a beautiful boy. He will be my son. Maybe I'll meet a woman who will mother him. Love him. I don't know how to care for him but she will. I'll do whatever it takes to give him a life. As soon as I get him into the cabin, I'll wrap warm blankets around him. I'll feed him root tea and potatoes until he gets his strength back. Then, we'll go to the city and find a restaurant where he can order whatever he wants. We will have a good time together.

I'm drifting. Losing strength. He comes closer with each wave, then moves away. He probably doesn't speak any English, except the one word his mother taught him. *Asylum, Asylum.* But he'll understand my love. He'll know my life is now devoted to caring for him. Just him. And, hopefully he'll soon have a new mother to hold him and kiss him. Must leave my hermit life and find a school for him. Over time, I will learn to be a good father, a loving father.

The closing lines from a Dylan Thomas poem come to me now: 'Time held me green and dying/Though I sang in my chains like the sea'. He is a beautiful boy. This orphan. I must save him. I will put him in my arms and carry him out of the cruel sea. For his sake! Not for the sake of Oliver Seawagon. The sea is near calm. Though I am weak, I feel alive for the first time in my life.

THE LEPRECHAUN

Jim woke up on the stoop with strands of tinsel rooted in his thick black hair, with a few pieces floating over his eyelids. The repetitive strains of *Happy Days Are Here Again* rang in his ears like persistent tinnitus. He tousled his hair and stepped down to the sidewalk. Nothing on the block looked familiar to him. Not sure if he was heading north, south, east or west, he walked for ten minutes until he saw evidence of commercial life. A hand-painted sign for Liquor/Wine drew him inside. With five dollars in his pocket, he bought a pint of Five Star Twister, leaving him $3.39 in change. Keeping the bottle tightly wrapped inside the brown paper bag, he unscrewed the cap and threw back a healthy swig as soon as he stepped outside. He stuffed the pint bottle into the inside pocket of his overcoat.

Five doors down from the liquor store, he saw the sign "HIRING NOW" in a storefront window. When he walked inside the one-room office, he encountered a man dressed in a three-piece suit seated behind a desk in the center of the room with stacks of papers spread over every inch of the metal surface. Without speaking, the man directed him to a row of chairs lined up against the wall. An old woman, seated at a desk opposite the chairs, took calls. When the phone stopped ringing, the telephone lady rose out of her chair and handed an application to Jim, a one-page form on a clipboard, a pencil tethered to it by a shredded piece of twine. She told him to fill it out as best he could.

The men who sat next to Jim were similarly dressed in scuffed shoes and donated overcoats two sizes too big. On the wall over their heads a neatly hand lettered sign read: Wittman's Employment Agency/FULL TIME/PART TIME/PER DIEM JOBS. The man seated on his right was fast asleep, head thrown back, snoring with his mouth wide open, revealing upper and lower rows of brown, rotted teeth. The man to his left anchored the heels of his shoes against the seat of the chair so that his crossed arms formed a shelf on top of his knees, where his head recovered from a difficult night. Every few minutes, the man's head would rise suddenly and each time he cast hollow stares at some point on the wall. Then his head would drop again to a resting position.

Jim filled out the application, writing down his parents' old address at 347 Cherry Street. He did not want the man to know his last known address was the Bowery Mission. When he got to the question that asked for employment history accompanied by the names of immediate supervisors, he left the space blank. When he finished, he rose and handed the paper to the man who looked it over quickly and asked, "I know times are tough out there but help me out, what kind of work do you do?"

"I cook and I box."

"I'm not sure I can help you with the boxing, but let me look ..." the man shuffled through several stacks of cards before he said, "Nothing for a cook ...". Picking out one card and looking up at Jim, he said "But would you be interested in doing something ... a bit unusual?"

"Like what?"

Scanning the application, he said, "James Callaghan. With a name like that you'd be perfect for this job."

"What kind of job?"

"It's a surprise birthday greeting for an eighty-year-old grandmother from her grandson who lives in Philly."

"So, I have to deliver a telegram or something like that?"

"Something like that. You have a nice speaking voice so what you'd be doing is reciting the message while wearing a handsome Irish leprechaun costume. And you look to be the right size for the one we have in stock. You knock on the old lady's door and read a special poem to her that her grandson wrote. You never know, she might even give you a tip on top of what we pay you. Looking better every minute, heh Callaghan?"

"Why the costume?" Jim said.

"She's Irish and the grandson said it'd be a hoot. She'll love it."

"That's not for me," Jim said, "Anything else you got in that stack?"

"Not right at this moment but ..."

As Jim started to rise out of his chair, the man said, "This job pays a hundred bucks, Callaghan. Where'ya gonna get that kind of money these days? Tell me."

Jim asked, "Does the cost of the costume come out of the hundred bucks."

"Nope. We provide the outfit. It's a crisp C-note for what ... an hour's work?"

"I don't know ..."

"We give you $50 cash up front and you come back here after the job is done for the balance when the costume is returned in good condition. We'll keep your clothes here and if you don't show up by tomorrow we'll deliver them to the address you put on the application. Easy money

Callaghan. Don't let it go. Where you going to get this kind of opportunity again?"

"My brother's got a steady job at New York Life. He never got laid off."

"Good for him. How much does he make a week?"

"Not sure. I think around twenty-five bucks … that was a while ago. Maybe he makes more now. I worked there a little while myself."

"You left that space blank. How come?"

"Bad luck. I was there two weeks when the market crashed."

"You want to make a career out of selling life insurance? Boring."

"I wasn't selling anything, just pushing paper around a desk like yours," Jim said.

"Boring," the man said.

The man behind the desk took out a scrap of paper and wrote some figures on it. He showed it to Jim, "See, you'd be making more than your brother already. You'd be getting four weeks salary in one day. One hour! Think about that. We get a good report about you from our client, I'll take a closer look through these other cards when you get back."

"How many leprechaun jobs you got lined up?"

"This is the only one at the present. You'd be a fool if you don't take it. Plenty of Irishers out of work, know what I'm saying?"

"Okay, I'll do it," Jim said.

The man opened the desk draw and pulled out two twenties and a ten, handing them to Jim. "Just sign this voucher which states I actually gave you half the payment we agreed to."

"My brother told me I should be thinking about my future."

"Let him think about his own future," the man said.

"Yeah, but I got to figure out what I'm going to do. You know, long term."

"Aren't we all in the same boat, Mr. Callaghan? You, me and those guys over there" the man said, as he thumbed through the stack of specialty jobs, "You know, after you come back I might have something else you can do."

"Where am I?" Jim said.

"What do you mean?"

"What street is this?

"You're sitting here on 3rd Avenue, off 33rd Street. Where the hell were you last night?"

"Some restaurant downtown."

"Well, you're on the right side of town now. This job is about fifty blocks north of where you're sitting. I'll give you a few extra bucks for a taxi."

"How do I know if the old lady's going to be home when I get there?"

"It's her 80th birthday, Callaghan. According to her grandson, she never leaves the apartment. Gets food delivered. Don't worry. She'll be there. By the way, don't let the message bother you. The grandson says she's got a great sense of humor and likes smutty stuff. My Grammy's a dirty old lady, he tells me. You're going to have a lot of fun with this one."

"So that's my future. Odd jobs? One day a leprechaun, next day a ..."

"Survivor, Callaghan. That's the business we're in. Survival. You Irish know all about that, don't you?"

"I'm an American."

"You got Irish blood, don't you?"

"For sure."

"Well, you can't bleed all the green out. Come into the back room with me. Try on the costume."

Jim donned the outfit and stuck the pint in the back pocket of the costume pants.

Jim stood on the corner of 33rd and 3rd wearing the Leprechaun outfit made out of velvet and taffeta fabrics. It consisted of a poplin cutaway tailcoat jacket with velvet collar and cuffs with decorative gold-tone buttons running up his chest and on the jacket cuffs. The vest front was velvet with a taffeta back. The knee pants over the light green stretch leggings had a button fly and elastic waistband. The black foam top hat was 8" high on his head and 21" around the brim. A scratchy ginger beard was looped with a band around his head.

Two taxi drivers slowed down when they saw Jim's raised hand but moved along when they got a closer look. A third cab stopped and Jim hopped in. During the ride, Jim drank more of the whiskey. The driver never stopped laughing until he delivered Jim to 382 East 81st Street.

The six-foot leprechaun walked into the building and up the stairs. He took one more Twister swig, then rang the bell of Apartment 2D. The birthday girl opened the door and glared at the man in the leprechaun outfit. "What the hell do you want?"

Jim stuck his soft, curled-up leprechaun shoe in the door and sang the birthday message in his best tenor voice:

I bring you a gift from afar
Hoping my voice scores a par.

THE NEXT MOTHER

Now listen to your birthday telegram:
Slam bam, thank you ma'am
Though you've been around the block at least twice
Knowing your love comes with a price
Just give me a chance
I got a bulge in my pants
You might be eighty today
But if I get my way
I'll pull down your skirt
N' you'll forget what hurts
With your nasty arthritis
(Lady tries to shut door on his foot. Jim finishes fast)
Because we'll be as tight as
A pig in a poke
Hey, it's all a joke
ON YOU
Happy Birthday Granny!

The woman grabbed the hat off his head as Jim scrambled for the staircase. He slipped on the floor as she screamed, "You pig. Who put you up to this?" She followed him to the edge of the steps as he struggled to get to his feet. While he was on all fours, she gave him a boot with her right foot and he tumbled end over end down the stairs boom, bam, boom like an empty trunk. The Five Twister bottle broke mid flight. He felt the liquid and pieces of glass on his backside. He reeked of cheap whiskey by the time he hit bottom. He scrambled to his feet and ran out of the building, Granny's piercing hollers for the police ringing in his ears.

He ran and ran, unaware in what direction he was headed. Feeling sick, he darted into a doorway and vomited. He wiped his mouth, ditched the fake beard and kept moving, heading south. Along the way, people pointed, and wished him a medley of Happy New Year, Happy Hallowe'en and Happy St. Patrick's Day.

He asked one passerby, "Where am I?"

"Why, you're in Ireland lad. This is the end of the rainbow and here's your pot of gold," the old man smiled as he tipped his hat and handed Jim loose change out of his pocket.

Jim made it a few more blocks and collapsed on the sidewalk. Three teenage boys came up to him and one of them said, "Youse in the wrong country, Mister." Another boy pitched pennies at him, and said, "Dis guy stinks. He needs a shower." The third boy started to piss on Jim's head but zipped it up and took off with his buddies when they saw a copper rushing toward them.

The cop gave Jim a whack on his wet behind with his nightstick, pushing pieces of glass deeper into his flesh, and told him to get up and keep it moving.

Jim made it as far as the Wittman Employment Agency. It was closed. It was getting dark and the temperature was dropping considerably. He blew into his hands and felt a few snowflakes fall on his face. He pressed his nose against the window. No sign of life inside. His overcoat, pants and shoes were in there. Somewhere.

The tips of his fingers and toes started to freeze up. He still had the $50 on him. Could get more bottles of Twister. That would warm him up. He remembered his clothes might be delivered to 347 Cherry but his parents won't be there. Their new address is in his overcoat somewhere in that office. On a napkin.

The snow fell heavier and thicker, sticking to his flimsy costume, soaking through to his skin. He headed to the Bowery Mission in his green jacket, bloody leggings and cloth shoes. Not included, the pot of gold.

He bought another pint. Got another Happy St. Patrick's Day from a passerby. A sorry looking leprechaun is he. Drank a third of the bottle in one gulp. The napkin with his brother Ray's number on it. The same napkin with his parents' new address on it. In his overcoat. At Wittman's.

Surely his parents will have some clothes for him. They sold the building and moved, Ray told him. The new owners. Can I look in the apartment for my clothes. Some might still be there. Get lost buster. Afraid to call Ray. Doesn't remember his number anyway. Call New York Life tomorrow. Is it a workday? What day is it? Walked down to Christie Street. Very dark. Heavy snow. Feet freezing worse than his hands. Freezing cold to the bone. Keep sipping. Sip. Sip. Feels sick again. Falls in the gutter. Gets up. Falls again.

Copper whacks him on the ass, tells him, "Hey Elf, you're a disgrace to the Irish. Keep moving, bum." Follows him. Whacks him again. More blood as more bits of glass press into his ass. Falls into gutter. Passes out. Cars push gray slush over his face and hands. Shivering. Lots of legs going by. No money left. Must've been robbed by some bum. Old script for medical hooch given to after he lost a fight. Maybe that's still good. In his overcoat. At Wittmans. Got to get there tomorrow. What day is it? Where am I? Poked along to Bowery by other nightsticks. Other coppers poke his ribs. Move. Move. I said MOVE you fucking bum!

Freezing December day. Frozen snot. Fingers blue. No feeling in toes. Teeth chattering like a trick wind-up set of choppers. Can't see a thing through the storm. Now heavy, sticking to everything. Begs for food. Needs dry clothes. Kind, tall red-headed copper runs him into the Mission. Singing some hymns. Gets in line for food. Can't just drink. Gotta eat. Want to be a bag of bones? Asks to spend the night. Not here. Sorry. Not tonight. Because of the cold. Full up. But I was just here yesterday. Had a bed. They offer food. Not hungry anymore, thank you. Feeling sick. Here's fifteen cents. Go up the street to the Washington Hotel for a bed. Come back here tomorrow, brother. When you're hungry for food. For the body. For the soul. Feed you ham, potatoes and Jesus. Want to know more about Jesus? Where am I? There's blood running down your tights. You'll get a nasty infection. Blood's coming out of your ass. Where am I? You're in the Bowery now. In a flophouse. With lovely chicken wire ceilings on top and cockroaches down below. See that rope over there. Lean over it with the others. Flop. Flop. Flop. When you're done puking, we'll get you a suite at the Palace. Don't worry about the stench or the mess. Don't get it on your shoes. Amos with the bucket cleans the floor but he doesn't do shoes. At least I'm working Amos says. If you want your own cell tomorrow night, go back on the street and beg for $2. If you get the $2 don't buy another pint. You'll die in the street sip, sip, sipping your life away. You'll be back in the gutter and the coppers'll stick you in the ribs, until you got holes in your chest and a black and blue behind. Welcome kid. You've hit the skid. Sing with us: *The Bowery, the Bowery, every city's got one and we call ours The Bowery, The Bowery.* Some call it NYC Skid Row.

We're like family here. We can pool our money and we'll all be better off. Wanna do that? Not sure. Where am I? You're in drunk-out-of-your-mind. This is the end of the line. The last outpost. The train don't go no further. Never made it to the Washington Hotel. What kind of shithole is this? I need another pint. A copper's nightstick in his gut. Know who I am, Callaghan? Hit the skids did you? Wouldn't your mother be proud. I missed my rent payment. Some time ago. I got another fifty bucks coming to me. I ain't got no clothes no more. Not sure what happened. I had a big fight. Big time $350 purse. If you got $350 I'll be you rmanager. What did you do with it? Where is it Callaghan? What's your name? Red Murphy. Lieutenant Red Murphy if that means anything to you. I met your brother at the big fight. Jungle Jim my ass. Another Irish brawler swinging at his father's face. Now here's a little whack on your ass to remember me by. Get out of the gutter. Keep moving. Next time I whack you it'll be your thick Irish head. Where can I get one little drink? You're asking the wrong person, Callaghan. Keep moving. If you stay in the gutter, another cop might not be so kind.

New York City is so lovely in a snowstorm. Flakes like crystals passing under the lamppost lights. Up and down the streets. Across the avenues. Glistening. Shimmering. Serene. Picture perfect. Hot cocoa smells so good, its swirl of steam flowing this way and that.

A NEW YORK ROMANCE

I was about six inches beneath the curb and sinking fast when Princess Nora from Andorra rescued me. That's Andorra Lane on Todt Hill, Staten Island, not the tiny country ruled by two nominal princes, and, oddly enough, a bishop.

Princess Nora's family emigrated to Staten Island from Andorra and bought a mansion on Old Farmer's Lane, with money they made on the vibrant tourism industry back home. Soon after they settled in, they changed the name of the Lane from Old Farmer's, which they considered stiff and farty sounding, to the present-day Andorra. Rather than go through all of the city's bureaucratic nonsense concerning this matter, they crafted their own handmade signs, then affixed them precisely on existing street signs up and down the lane.

The neighbors did not mind at all since the new signs were quite handsome, replete with old world calligraphic lettering, antique looking in a classic pre-war semi art nouveau Andorran, European kind of way. Their appearance reminded some Todt Hill residents of the signs situated at Metro stations in Paris, not surprisingly, as Andorrans have a lot of French blood coursing through their veins. Besides, the well-heeled, sophisticated neighbors on Old Farmer's, now unofficially Andorra, did not want to tangle with this family because of their volatile DNA cocktail mix of Catalan, Spanish and French heritage. On an even brighter side, the more *nouveau riche* inhabitants of Todt

Hill never miss an opportunity to haughtily boast about residing in the city's only known Andorran enclave. It comes as no surprise that Princess Nora herself is consistently invited to formal Todt Hill gatherings. She never goes unnoticed, strikingly bearing the exquisite visage of a French beauty queen, the ample hips of a Spanish maiden and the salty tongue of a Catalan separatist.

Before I met the Princess, I tried everything that I felt dwelt within my giftedness. I went truckin' on the West Side Highway the day it caved in, subsequently killing a few unsuspecting cats and dogs on the ground below. I was voted Homecoming King of Greenwich Village in 1968. I tried sex, violence, drugs and lots of booze. I even tried Steve's Luncheonette on Fulton Street in Brooklyn. I had brains, balls and beer but very little capital, at least not enough to even consider courtin' a member of royalty such as the beautiful and elegant Princess Nora. Though lowly in birthright, originally domiciled in my toddler years in the Bronx, I was determined to raise myself up to ever-higher levels.

Never one to brag, I am a card-carrying member of several prestigious societies, although I am not sure that the Princess would have been impressed with their regality as they are very clandestine and totally off limits to persons of the female gender. In fact, no one outside of these societies has any idea what they stand for. No records are kept of our meetings. Information is warehoused within our heads and passed down from father to son, uncle to nephew. Namely, I am proud to admit active membership in The Ancient Mystic Order Bagmen of Baghdad Hibernian Guild, The American Virility Society, and the Military Order of the Cootie Supreme Four Man Tent.

It was at the annual convention in Paris for this latter group where I saw Princess Nora for the first time. On s break from some very important conferences, I was sitting on a bench on the Champs-Elysees very near L'Arc de Triomphe when I looked up from the current French edition issue of *Mad* magazine that I was fervently studying and saw her.

Actually, it was the second time I beheld her exquisite beauty. Previously, I spotted her on the transatlantic flight, soon after our departure from JFK airport. I caught a fleeting glimpse of her as the flight attendant pulled back the curtain separating first class from us plebeians and there she stood in all her regal splendor.

I do not know how they managed to do it, but Pan Am did not provide the steerage section of the aircraft with air conditioning. Feeling quite uncomfortable and claustrophobic, I foolishly tried to roll down the window at 33,000 feet and got sucked out as we were making our descent into Orly Airport. Amazingly, my ill-fitting Good Will purchased jacket billowed as I fell to earth. I landed safely on the left bank of the Seine and, to everyone who knows, the left bank is far less dangerous than the right. It was my lucky day, I guess.

In between breakout sessions at the convention, I tried other, more daring things. For one, I attempted to tutor Charles de Gaulle's illegitimate children but I found them to be quite dense, obtuse even, so it was difficult for me to get through to them on any level. They were twins, a boy and a girl, very de Gaullish. I guess you'd have to say they were fraternal twins, but that doesn't sound right because the girl could not be his brother. Sorority twins then, just to be fair. However, they were identical twins when they played hooky from home school and dressed up like dad. They were both exceptionally tall just like dad and looked smashing in military uniforms and those iconic squarish General de Gaulle hats. You would swear they were identical. They had very big noses, just like dad. They were very proud to be his children although he never laid claim to them, nor did he ever bother to visit them, at least not during school hours. Sometimes when they got dressed up like dad, they would sing silly songs with verses like 'Vive le Quebec libre'.

Let us now make an Algerian pancake' and other lyrics in French which I could hardly understand because I only know about three words in that language. Maybe that's why I found it difficult to get through to them. After a while, I quit that gig. The francs were good but I lost my taste. Other than that futile effort I tried intellectualism, hand painting postcards and radical politics, all quite trendy in the late 1960's.

Princess Nora did not rescue me in Paris, however. When the fateful day came that we first encountered one another, I was unable to get the lump out of my throat in order to utter barely one intelligible enough syllable that would indicate to her that I was in desperate need of help. However, just a few days later, Princess Nora did rescue me in Madrid, where I took a much-needed holiday following a very tense and contentious convention amongst my formidable Cootie Four Man Tent colleagues. I was sitting in some godforsaken café on Gran Via one arid afternoon in late August and could not for the life of me get the attention of any of the arrogant Spanish waiters for what seemed like upwards of several hours when she fulfilled her princessly duties, scolded the entire café staff in her imperious Catalan tongue and got me a cold soda herself, fetched out of a nearby vending machine that sold Cokes and condoms. Europe, at that time, was way ahead of the curve.

Aside from the annoyance of having to pay a capping fee, I had the presence of mind and heart to overlook the shrewd pettiness of the café staff and instantly fell in love with her. I will never forget that day, much less the heavenly experience. We looked at each other, peered into each other's very souls, and swore right then and there that we would never again go to another bullfight once we returned to the States. She saved me from the inferno in Hell's Kitchen where I lived at the time. It was there, in that haven of mean tempers and bloody, sacrificial lambs and rabbits hanging in every butcher shop window, that the median income remained stagnant at a mere $30,000 per annum and also where two Christmas trees shed their needles in every 9' x 12' shaggy living room.

Yes, I knew it was true love when I would wake up at two a.m. every morning and wait several hours for the never on time number X9 bus to take me and two other passengers over the Verrazano Bridge to her palace on Staten Island in the exclusive Todt Hill enclave. I used to gloat over the fact that all my High School buddies were all stuck dating the original BIC pens – Bronx Irish Catholic girls - required to wear itchy blue knee socks and madras Bermuda skorts even in January, whereas I was dating a rich, aristocratic Princess from the Island of Staten, often referred to as the forgotten borough.

I was penniless at the time, empty of heart and longing for a meaningful human relationship instead of being kept captive with a stupid canary inherited from my dead aunt. The she or he bird would only sing when I relieved myself in the bathroom. Depending on the length of the process, the bird would sometimes perform an entire opera.

For certain, Princess Nora put me in touch with the finer things in life. It was she who told me to place the linen napkin on my lap and not tuck it into my shirt, and that Prince Igor's Polesvetskian Dances was composed by Alexandr Borodin, not that pretentious Englishman who died six months before he shilled for classical Columbia Records on Channels 5, 9, and 11. It was she who introduced me to cuchifritos, pastellas, arroz compoyo, pate de foie gras, escargot and Johnny Rodriquez whose marimba band is still playing our song.

It was Princess Nora who convinced me not to move to Pittsburgh and instead simply order a Pizzaburger on Hyland Boulevard, where you've tried the rest, now try the best. I knew it was true love when the S73 bus finally got me to George Street and I would walk several miles to her castle. And in the twilight hours between night and morning under a pale, misty moon I would gently toss love pebbles and dirt bombs at her window until I found out it was her mother's window who one night dropped the rope ladder to the ground and asked me to elope with her because her husband was driving her crazy with his snoring and sordid tales of when he was a nasty, little bandito in a tiny village of an underdeveloped country in South America. Worse than that, he started taking an interest in his wife's clothing, raiding her wardrobe closet periodically. One day, he found an outfit he really liked, probably a leftover costume ball outfit, a kind of Cleopatra short dress, day-glow lime green complete with a gilt, braided cloth belt, and a cheap plastic tiara with half of the brassy looking surface peeling off.

One day he wore that outrageous costume (without underwear) on an antiquing junket to the most exclusive shops on the east side of Manhattan. Just to add to the bizarre nature of the whole trip, he was caught red handed urinating in one shop's Ming or Bling dynasty urns. When confronted, he protested that he innocently thought urn was short for urinal. He got away with that once but at another shop, he repeated this offensive behavior, which there are laws against, and challenged the police by saying, of course it is a urinal, where else could we find in the English language, words with the letters u-r-n so close together. A very sharp, New York City detective with an Irish name like McClafferty, McCaffrey, or McAfee, answered him by saying I got two words for you, 'turn around' upon the obedience of said command, Nora's father was handcuffed and taken away. Nora's Mom bailed him out and started to plan her escape.

Yes, now I have all that I hoped and dreamed for, a beautiful home with several light bulbs still working, a country church on the corner, designer trash cans that teenagers knock over every Thursday night, two fresh kids who will get whatever they want until my Visa card is cancelled, two cars I cannot afford the snow tires for, a next door neighbor who sues every bastard innocently tripping down Hyland Boulevard, and personal loans that are cosigned by everyone including my fifteen year old niece who agreed to have her weekly allowance garnisheed for the next twenty two months. When you get right down to it, I am just a happy suburban househusband cursed with garlic breath who is stuck with the albatross of an Irish heritage in search of the perfect Andorran pearl – raw material at best, a gem in the rough, a terror in the nude, put away in the tax shelter for battered husbands by an out of touch with reality princess who cannot tell if she is exacerbating or ameliorating the cause for women's rights by staying married to this terribly confused, totally disoriented nut on the loose whose sole purpose is to test her love every minute and every hour of every day who himself will stay in love with her forever and ever despite her fervent prayers to the contrary.

THE NEXT MOTHER

Several of the working girls tried to chase down the big red rig as it pulled into an open spot at BIG STOP. The towering neon Fuel/Eats/Showers sign blinked upon a flashed fishnet stocking here and an exposed breast there. Decisions had to be made quickly on such a cold December night. The winners of the race, as the radiant fire red Peterbilt 579 hissed to a full stop, were two flat chested women who looked like desperate malnourished waifs in the rear-view mirror. They jumped on the step rail and swung the door open so fast, Bill had no time to discourage them. He came to the Route 80 stop for coffee and a meal. They came for something else.

The driver behind the wheel soon found out they were not truck stop hookers but a mother-daughter team dressed only in rough muslin dresses and headscarves. They were dropped off at this central Pennsylvania location just an hour earlier, told by the van driver they would be picked up by another carrier who would take them on the final leg of their long journey to a safe, friendly, and warm haven, unlike any other they ever experienced in their entire lives.

Independent owner-operator Bill Reynolds looked down at the dark skinned and frail females, thinking, 'well, what do we have here'. He flicked on the interior light to observe the expression on the mother's face. It told a story of pain rather than anger, resignation more than revenge. Big Bill Reynolds never felt so small in his big rig than on this occasion. This might be the end, he intuitively thought, at least on this particular night, to all the pleasures he looks forward to at BIG STOP, a refueling oasis for truck and man. He wished he had pulled into a stop closer to home in Clarion, or even legged it out further east to get weighed in, dieseled up, fed, showered and serviced as he hauled another load of barrels, bolts and screws from one section of the country to another. It was the girl, more so than her mother, who spoiled everything. This was no place for a minor. What kind of mother would take her child out on a night like this, clothing her in such a flimsy garment?

Mada knew it was coming the day her friend, Shaista, told her to leave. With a dirty cloth sack slung over her shoulder, Shaista banged on Mada's door, yelling, "The soldiers are coming. Leave everything behind and follow us!" Villages on either side of them were under attack. The smoke smelled thick, near and noxious. It was only a matter of time. Leave now or you will die. Shaista's husband, tightly clutching their infant son, commanded her to follow him. She ran to him as they fled to the forest.

Bill knew the sleeper compartment in his Peterbilt would remain vacant on this particular visit. He saved all of his adult life so he could buy the truck of his dreams, a massive 579 model that would rule the road. Aside from all the top-of-the-line mechanical features, the bunk accommodated an eighty-two-inch mattress, the largest in the industry. He and his wife Tricia would always have a place to stay when they were on the road. She was excited about the idea at first, but had yet to join him on any of his trips. Something always came up. Too expensive to board the dogs. Her mother needs her. All sorts of excuses kept the sheets on their mobile marriage bed clean and fresh.

Mada looked up at Bill, her stolid expression unchanged. She had a small body and was able to put some distance between Bill and herself. She had not spoken one word from the moment she climbed into the cab. Mahfuzah, her back turned away from the adults, broke the silence, "Are you angel?"

"No, I'm Bill," he said, "What is your name?" Neither one of them answered.

"Is this your mother?" he asked, "Can she speak?"

"No," the girl said, still facing the dark world outside the truck.

"I want to let you know I'm not going to hurt either one of you," Bill said, even though the women could have fled the moment they sensed any harm coming their way. They were keenly aware of the difference between danger and safety.

Bill saw he had a clear view of the top of their heads. Only wisps of their dark hair were visible outside the headscarves. When Mada noticed that Bill was staring at their heads, she bent forward and pulled back her scarf far enough so that Bill could see the thick, deep scars on her scalp which no amount of hair could obscure. She then gently turned her daughter around and pushed back her head covering. Bill stared at the girl's head. She also had deep scars on her scalp, nearly identical to her mother's. Both women pulled their headscarves back into place.

"Look, " Bill said quietly, "I'm not the person you think I am."

Staring straight at the trucker, still expressionless, Mada's eyes welled up, then the tears flowed down her face. Bill grabbed a tissue. Unafraid, Mada allowed him to wipe her tears. Bill noticed that her face still appeared moist. He formed a V with his forefinger and middle finger and gently traced the exact tracks where the tears rolled down from her eyes, over her dark, prominent cheeks. Bill sensed that the woman knew the big truck driver would not hurt her so she let him examine her face. Bill appreciated her exotic beauty, which reminded him of a Polynesian contestant he once saw in a Miss World pageant, quite unlike the women he was familiar with in western Pennsylvania.

As he sat in his beloved Peterbilt truck, with its custom-built bunk designed for merrymaking on the lonely open road, he knew his friends would mercilessly mock him for picking up two females at a truck stop who were not prostitutes from who knows what part of the world and one of them a preteen, no less. And they wore headscarves.

Bill thought the mother was once beautiful, with a broad forehead, high cheekbones, a finely formed nose, with the darkest, deepest eyes he'd ever seen. Certainly like nothing he had ever encountered in the Clarion mall.

The young girl did not have her mother's looks. Maybe she took after her father. Bill considered these things while he evaluated his current situation. If he ever told his bar buddies about the circumstance he currently found himself in, he could predict one of them would say, 'did you bang the daughter too'.

The practical half of his brain began telling him to kick the ladies out of his truck and start haulin' ass to Massachusetts to drop his load while the roads were still mostly empty. The other half spelled out adventure, maybe even accompanied by risk and danger. Let's see where all this leads, he thought.

Bill had to make some kind of stay or go decision. He could simply fork over a few bucks and tell them to be on their way. Yet, he felt compelled to find out why the mother went through the trouble of showing her scars to him, and her daughter's. She must want to tell him their story. He was intrigued enough to at least find out, not knowing whether that information would lead to more involvement on his part.

Throughout most of central Pennsylvania, snowflakes fell sporadically from a gray sky, disappearing before they reached the ground. The weather forecast over the radio was a stark warning to Bill that he had a small window where he had to decide whether to go back home or make the run immediately from western Pennsylvania to Springfield, Massachusetts.

Bill invariably favored starting his journeys late at night and timed it so that he was able to partake of all the amenities available 24/7 at his favorite BIG STOP off Route 80. But matters were complicated at the moment, sitting side by side with two strange females. He was not sure what he should do. He felt like calling Tricia to get her advice but it would annoy her getting a call like that so late at night. She would have all sorts of relevant questions to ask him which he was not presently equipped to answer.

Bill knew he could tell Tricia anything, whatever was on his mind, and she felt likewise. They struggled mightily in the early stages of their marriage, ever since she lost their only child due to complications during pregnancy. They never tried to have another child after that. But over the course of their fifteen-year marriage, she and Bill grew closer together. Through intensive bereavement and couples counseling, they felt they had a healthy dependency on one another. Bill decided not to call his wife just yet. He would try to figure out things on his own, whatever the outcome.

"What's going on?" Bill asked Mada, then turned to the daughter, "Why won't she answer me?"

"No hear your words. No speak your words," she said.

"Is she deaf and dumb?"

"No. Muslim," the girl answered.

"What's her name?" Bill said.

"Mada."

"She is your mother, right?"

"Yes."

"What's your name?" Bill asked the girl. He then looked directly at Mada, pointing to the daughter, "What is her name?"

"Mahfuzah" she answered proudly.

Bill gently tapped Mahfuzah on the shoulder and said, "You see. She does understand me."

"Not much," Mahfuzah said.

"Will you let me help you?" Bill said softly to Mada.

Mada moved her face closer to Bill's, with tears again welling up in her eyes, and said, "Yes. Please."

Several days later, their infant son Muhammad had slept on Mahfuzah's lap, her husband Raheel and their six-year-old son Arfan gathered firewood for the evening meal. Frightening screams were heard from thirty huts away. The stench of burning flesh spread throughout the village. The screams grew louder and were coming nearer.

Bill heard a tapping on his side of the truck. He opened the window and saw the truck stop preacher man holding an old school blackboard pointer, rigged with a metal tip. The preacher used it to get the attention of the truckers, sitting so high up in their cabs. "Now is not a good time," Bill told him.

"It's always a good time, Joe."

"My name is Bill."

"Son, there is no time like the present to turn over your life to the Lord."

"I am not your son, and like I just said, now is not a good time, Padre." Bill could see that the self-appointed chaplain of BIG STOP was not easily discouraged. Wearing a clerical collar, the clergyman regularly checked on the truckers parked in the waiting area. He rarely spoke to the harvest field hookers, however ripe for picking.

"If I give you a Bible, Joe, will you promise to read it and to share it with the ladies?" the minister said in calm, measured tones, unable to make eye contact, for the strain evangelizing put on his neck.

"Are you hard of hearing? I said this is not a good time. There is something else going on right here."

"That's just it, son. I know exactly what's going on and that's why I'm talking to you. The time for salvation for you and the ladies is now."

"I don't think these ladies would be too receptive to your message at the moment."

"I know the power of God's Holy Word," the minister said, looking up.

"You know nothing," Bill said impatiently, " Go to the next truck. Joe is nearer to hell and damnation than I am."

"You know this for sure, son?"

"Oh yes, for sure," Bill said with finality.

The minister moved along with his testament and pointer to the next truck. The girl, who witnessed the exchange, smiled at Bill.

Both Raheel and Mada came from poverty so their wedding was modest by necessity yet was rich with promises, that they each kept throughout their marriage. On their wedding day, Raheel gave Mada a fresh date that they ate together. He promised that he would never marry another woman, that he would always love and protect her from harm and be a good father to their children, also promising them love and protection with the same commitment and determination.

Mada promised to be a faithful wife, and a devoted mother to the many children she knew Raheel wanted her to bear. Raheel's older brother Jaah officiated at the wedding and read the *Fatihah*, the first book of the Quran, offering blessings to each of them. Mada stayed in Shaista's hut until it was time to sign the *Nikah*. For the *meher*, Raheel gave Mada a necklace made of small wood hearts that he carved and strung together on a strip of leather. In the *meher*, Raheel stated that he would add to the necklace, with a carved figure representing each newborn child, which would be interlaced in such a way that the figure of each child would rest between two hearts.

Bill was still undecided what to do. He took a one hundred dollar bill out of his wallet and handed it to Mada. She refused. Mahfuzah spoke to her mother in Arabic, insisting that she take the money. They needed to find a place to sleep that night. Bill put the bill back in his wallet and invited them to join him in the cafeteria for a meal.

The women followed him into the building. While they were in line, pushing their trays along the rack and trying to decide which foods would be acceptable to eat, Bill excused himself and went to the magazine and souvenir shop just steps away. He hurriedly purchased two

Keystone State sweatshirts. He tried to think of what else he could do in the short amount of time he had left before he needed to get back on the road to get ahead of the approaching storm. The snowflakes, previously light and airy, now fell with thicker flakes, accumulating on the ground.

After they sat down to their meal, Bill excused himself again, telling them he had to use the men's room. There, he planned to call Tricia to let her in on what he sensed was a crisis for these two women. The voicemail picked up after three rings but Bill thought it best to say nothing.

When Bill returned to the table, the women were not there, leaving their brand new Keystone State sweatshirts draped over a chair with the price tags still intact. Their meals were half eaten, teabags limply hanging off the edges of their cups. Frantic, Bill asked other truckers nearby if anyone had seen them. They shrugged their shoulders.

He ran outside, going from truck to truck to see if the mother and daughter were still looking for their angel. He did not understand why they would leave without telling him.

The snow started to fall more steadily. His fellow truckers were either asleep or bedding down with the last of the hookers who no longer had any interest in freezing by pulling down their tops. None of the working girls were in sight. Frustrated, he headed back into the cafeteria.

Only a handful of truckers occupied the long, communal tables in the hall, fortifying themselves with meatloaf, mashed potatoes with gravy and buttered bread, needing to hit the road, with nothing on their minds but to start'er up and get'er moving. He belonged to that club, of men who favor the loneliness of the open road, the solitude of a brightly lit cafeteria, and the ping ping of the arcade pinball machines the BIG STOP owners installed to make a few extra bucks.

After his frantic search, Bill saw mother and daughter peacefully finishing their meal. As he approached the table, Mada stood up and bowed to him. Mahfuzah did the same. After a long discussion in the ladies room, Mada decided to share with her daughter that this big trucker man could be trusted, that he was someone they could tell their story to. Mahfuzah trusted her mother's judgment. Since neither one of them could carry on a conversation in English, as Mada knew nothing of the language, and Mahfuzah capable of only a few expressions here and there, Mada suggested that they tell their story to the trucker in pictures.

Bill asked Mahfuzah how he could be of help. The young girl said "Tell story," and motioned with her hand the act of drawing. Bill asked them to wait, awkwardly pantomiming his intentions. The decision was made to forgo the trip to Massachusetts.

The snow fell quite heavily now, bolstered by a blustery wind. As Bill left the cafeteria to fetch the yellow pad, and whatever pens and pencils were scattered about in his truck, he saw the last handful of fellow truckers line up for diesel fuel, preparing to make a run for their own payday destinations.

The wind blew the snow across the tall lamplights in the parking lot. The big storm the experts predicted, was heading their way. As he re-entered the cafeteria, there was just a smattering of truckers, most of them getting ready to leave, ordering large size coffees to go. Bill got a coffee for himself and tea for mother and daughter. He sat down with them at the long, communal table. He pushed the pad over to Mada, supplying her with several pens and pencils. Mada stared at the blank page for several minutes. There is so much she had to tell this man but could not do it justice in just one drawing. She needed to extract from that pen in her hand a realistic delineation of what actually happened to her, her daughter and the other members of her family.

She stared at the page. Bill nudged the cup of tea closer to her elbow, encouraging her to drink. Mahfuzah did not look at her mother's attempts to draw. She got out of her chair, knelt on the cement floor, placed her head on her mother's lap, and wept the entire time her mother spoke with each stroke of her pen. She knew the story. She was right at the heart of it.

Mada finished the first drawing pushing the pad across the table to Bill.

Mada knew of other villages, not that far away, that were pillaged and burned to the ground, but she felt safe. Raheel had promised to protect her and the children. He always kept his promises. After Shaista warned her, having no reason to believe her friend would ever lie or even exaggerate, she stepped outside to see for herself. Her home was on a bit of a rise, so she looked south, over the tops of her neighbors' homes and saw the smoke and flames rising from one hut. A few minutes later, more flames reached for the sky from another hut, then another. It was time to run. Where were Raheel and Arfan?

"Is this your village?" Bill asked of Mada. She nodded affirmatively, pointing to one of the huts, not burning. "Your home?" he asked. Mada nodded again.

"No more," Mahfuzah whispered, her soft voice muffled within the folds of her mother's lap. Mada hoped that her daughter would fall asleep, rather than have to relive the horrors of their trauma. Although no words were spoken, in English or Arabic, the mother knew with certainty that Mahfuzah was fully aware and could predict with clairvoyant accuracy the subject matter of each drawing that was yet to come from her mother's mind and hand, and knew with the same degree of accuracy the order in which they would be drawn.

Bill placed the first drawing face down on the table. Mada stared at the blank page. Her mind wandered for a moment. She was not striving for a dramatic flourish but considered that this form of story-telling might be even more truthful, more accurate than the spoken word, only because, if she were required to tell her story verbally, she would be tempted to blurt it out in one big rush of words, to get it over with, despite the inevitable interruptions filled with fits of sobbing. Still, feeling inadequate that it had to be done this way, she convinced herself that it was nevertheless the best available method of communication, for this subject and for this encounter with a total stranger.

Mada stared at the blank page for several minutes. She fingered the array of pens and pencils Bill had fetched from the truck. For this next drawing, she chose a pencil and a red pen. She began to draw, then put the pencil down for a moment, staring off to the other side of the hall, in the direction of another trucker. She made note of his garments, the apparel of a deer hunter, boots laced up to mid-calf, military-style camouflage pants tucked inside of them.

Where was Raheel who promised to protect her? Mada waited in the hut until she could wait no more. She grabbed whatever clothing she could and asked Mahfuzah to carry her baby brother. Her husband and other son would join them later. She began to draw.

One soldier, holding a rifle across his chest, stood in the doorway blocking their exit. Mada could see some of what was taking place outside the front door through the narrow opening of the man's bent arm. Then she heard her husband's voice before he came into view. He yelled, "Run Mada. Run!" Standing on her tiptoes, straining to look over the man's shoulder, she saw three other soldiers lead Raheel and Arfan to a tree, just thirty feet outside the hut. They stretched her husband's thin arms around the young tree, binding his hands with rope. Arfan clung to his father's feet, pleading for the soldiers to stop. One soldier tried to tear the boy away but the six-year-old gripped his father's leg even tighter. It was the only safe and protective place he knew. When the soldier could not dislodge the boy's arms, he withdrew a long knife from its sheath, which was looped on his belt and tied with a leather strip around his thigh. With one hand, the soldier held the boy's curly black hair. With his other hand, he slit the boy's throat. Arfan's body slithered to the ground. The soldier wiped the bloody residue dripping off the steel blade onto Arfan's soiled shorts. As Raheel looked down to witness the swift murder of his eldest son, his mouth opened wide, letting loose a high-pitched scream. From twenty feet away another soldier took aim, firing a bullet into Raheel's chest. With deadly accuracy, the bullet pierced his heart. His body slumped to the ground, falling on top of his son. Mada rushed over to Mahfuzah and Muhammad, attempting to cover them with her body. Mahfuzah did not see everything her mother saw but when the soldier moved away from the open doorway and tackled Mada before she could reach her children, the ten-year old girl saw her father and brothers' bodies on the ground, covered in blood.

Mada was exhausted after the execution of the second drawing. Mahfuzah felt her mother's body shake in one continuous undulating sigh. She wrapped her arms around her mother's waist and held on tight.

Bill took the drawing from Mada's hands, held out to him as a sacrificial offering. He examined the drawing and its fiercely scribbled red ink jottings of blood. He placed it face down on top of drawing number one, then stood up, looked down with deep sadness upon the shaking mother and daughter whose face was buried in her mother's lap, her whole body heaving, whimpering like an abandoned puppy.

Bill wanted to place his large hands on the mother and daughter's shoulders to comfort them but held back. Instead, he put his hand in his pocket, jingled loose change, not knowing what else to do. Restless, he walked around the long table a few times, stretching his legs as mother and daughter did their best to comfort one another upon having to revisit the experiences that would haunt their lives forever. How much more was forthcoming, he had no idea, but suspected it would be a great deal worse than what he had already surmised from the simple, yet stark interpretations of the murdered innocents.

The vast, wide-open hall with its vaulted ceiling felt cold and too brightly lit for such a dark tale to unfold. Mada stroked her daughter's hair and found enough strength to sketch the next scene.

The soldier who had been guarding the door tackled Mada from behind, in the process violently ripping the necklace made of small hand carved wood hearts and baby profiles from her neck. Mahfuzah's instinct was to hold her baby brother tightly. She screamed for help but the only living things that came through the door were the three soldiers who just shot her father and slit her brother's throat. An insidious chorus of screams and rapid-fire gunshots rang throughout the village as more and more huts were attacked by a marauding army of soldiers brutally assaulting unarmed villagers.

Mada and Mahfuzah were totally besieged by the horror the soldiers inflicted upon them. Now, there were four men inside their hut. No escape was possible. One of the soldiers ripped the clothing off Mada as she vainly tried to reach her surviving children. She was pinned to the ground. One man knelt on her left arm, another on her right, a third held her legs fast to the floor and spread them apart as the fourth soldier unzipped his fly, knelt down and raped the helpless mother.

Mahfuzah hit the soldier nearest her on the back of his head. He arose and punched her full force on the side of her face, knocking her unconscious to the floor. The same man then picked up the infant by one of his legs, walked outside the doorway and spun around several times in the manner of a hammer-throw athlete, before releasing the child skyward. The baby sailed through the air then its tiny body fell to the rock-strewn ground with an ugly thud.

Mada had looked over her shoulder to witness this horror and screamed. The other three men took turns raping her and slapping her so she would be silenced. When she tried to get to her feet, one of her attackers bludgeoned her on the head with his machete, leaving her for dead. While Mahfuzah was still in a semi-conscious state, one of the soldiers ripped the clothing off the then ten-year old girl and raped her then struck her head with a machete. The men straightened out their pants, closed the door behind them and set fire to the hut.

The tears flowing down Mada's face that Bill had witnessed in the truck, now came full force as her eyeballs rolled in their sockets revealing only the whites of her eyes, her head bobbed back and forth like a heavy weight resting on a coiled spring. Mahfuzah helped her mother walk to the ladies room. Mahfuzah, only eleven but physically strong, supported her mother, totally sapped of any strength.

Mada wished she was capable of depicting each scene more completely, if only she possessed some degree of artistic talent, so that what actually took place could be explicitly portrayed in the fullness of its frightening horror.

Mada did not ask her daughter to draw. She wanted to protect her above all else, hoping some day that the terrors her daughter tragically witnessed would not ruin her future life, hoping that some day she could go to school, meet a faithful man like her father and try to put the past behind her.

Mada lay awake most nights since these atrocities happened and knew that her beloved daughter, at least for the short term, would not sleep in peace, as she was always twitching, turning about and often screaming herself awake.

Bill looked at the big clock on the wall. It was four thirty in the morning, much too early to call his wife. He would not pressure Tricia to help the two refugees, who were racked with emotional and psychological pain, but he at least wanted his wife to hear their story as depicted in the graphic drawings.

By six a.m., he decided to give her a call and explain why he was not halfway to Massachusetts. Other than a decent income and a modest home, he realized that there was little he brought to their marriage. He did not want to introduce any new trouble into their lives. He had no idea as yet what he wanted to propose to her and made no plans to rehearse what to say to her. He only wished that she listen to what he had experienced from ten o'clock the previous evening throughout the entire night.

Not one given to self-examination, Bill felt a seismic change charging through his mind and spirit. Not once since he and his young bride lost their baby, did he require of himself any kind of deep thinking. At that time they were both determined to save their marriage before it all fell apart. This trip turned out to be a major gut check for big Bill and no one would be more surprised than he at how determined he was to consider his own place in this troubled world, much less troubled for him than for the women providing an eyewitness account to unimaginable personal tragedy.

Mada and Mahfuzah returned to the table. Bill stood up as they approached and held out their chairs for them. To his surprise, Mahfuzah reached for the yellow pad and a pencil. Her mother tried to take it away from her but she persisted, telling Mada that she also has a story to tell, that will not duplicate or contradict her mother's but will offer her own perspective of the degradation and the loss. Mada spoke sharply to her daughter. She took the pad and pencil out of her hands, then looked at Bill as if to ask for support.

"Mahfuzah," Bill said gently, "I am so sorry. You don't have to say anything else."

Mahfuzah shook her head vigorously and blurted out,

"My story," and pointed to the scars on her scalp. Mada touched her daughter's face and pushed the pad and pencil in her direction.

The young girl bent her head over the blank page, stared at it for several minutes, then jerked her head up and suddenly screamed. The cafeteria workers and the few customers remaining in the hall were startled by the outburst and looked over in that direction. Bill waved his hand. Everything's okay he said , go back to what you were doing. Mahfuzah again bent over the pad, broke the pencil in two and pounded her fist on the table. Mada and Bill gave her free rein. They were there for support, but each worried what torment the eleven-year-old was bringing upon herself at this exact moment.

Whatever Mahfuzah planned to write would have to wait. Mada took the pad back and immediately began another drawing.

Her head bleeding, the hut engulfed in fire, Magda placed her torn blouse on top of her wound, putting pressure on it. She crawled over to Mahfuzah, placed her head on her daughter's chest, reassured she heard a beating heart. She hesitated because her own heart was beating so rapidly. Is that what she was hearing? Her own heart? She opened Mahfuzah's mouth, placed her nose in the opening. She felt her daughter's soft breath entering her nostrils. She knew her daughter was still alive. She dragged her over to the back window, away from the fire raging in front and tied a cloth over her head. She struggled to get the window open, then smashed it with the chair, desperately clearing away glass shards off the bottom rim of the frame. She maneuvered her daughter's body in such a way so the girl was propped up in a sitting position, with her back resting against the wall beneath the window. Mada climbed out of the window, then lifted the girl and carried her in her bruised arms, both half naked, rushing, without looking at the bodies of her two sons and husband. They ran into the woods to safety.

Exhausted, feeling the pinch of strained muscles, she stopped several times to catch her breath, hearing her daughter's moans, telling her repeatedly, "We live. Praise Allah. We live. We will never be apart." She hoped to reach the river where all the village mothers washed their clothes, praying incessantly that it was low tide so they could cross to the other side and journey to another country. Her body, totally spent, could go no further. Mentally and physically drained of all energy, her legs lacking the strength to push further, she lay down on the soft forest loam, placed Mahfuzah's body in the cradle of her arms and fell into a deep slumber, with no time to weep.

There would be no tears until the shock wore off but when the tears did come, they would not stop; they would flow until there was no more liquid in the eyes, then the tears would turn into involuntary bodily heaves, a wrenching of the spirit and the desire to die rather than live one more minute in a world that would permit such cruelty. The tears would stain her face.

Mada looked at her daughter and knew she must continue, at least to give her the opportunity to live in some other part of the world where people were kind and loving. Everything that just happened put them in a state of shock. What they saw and what they experienced did not happen, could not happen. It had to be the stuff of a frightening nightmare. The torture and cruelty took place so quickly and so thoroughly, that they could not be real. Whatever took place fell into the black hole of depravity. It became the eddy that whirled dirt, betrayal, violence, man's sin, government indifference, the abuse of power in a dizzying flurry of cancerous evil. The acts of the ruling class were just too extreme to be real. Yet, because the rapes and assassinations were so extreme, Mada for the time being could not think of anything else but escape, to ward off any further violence to her surviving daughter. What might happen throughout the remainder of her life or her daughter's life could never again have such depth of horror, of misfortune, of nightmarish depravity. In an instant, Mada decided to combat the extreme with an extreme effort to save her daughter, not only from future physical and sexual harm, but from the torment of an ongoing tortured mind, a mind that could not and would not survive what defiled her, that shamed her by being treated more lowly than an animal butchered live for the feast.

The extreme defilement already began to harden Mada against whatever the world had yet to offer, took away any feeling of discomfort or shame about her nakedness in pursuit of escape, and survival. That is why she could lie on a cold and damp forest floor and not feel the cold or the dampness. Her mind, heart and spirit declared war against the evil spirits that demonstrated the willingness to take anything else away from her. She would fight for Mahfuzah and herself. Fight to the death.

This was the last drawing Mada would do this day, exhausted and drained all over again, her muscles remembering the ache and fatigue, the torn walls of her vagina still pulsating, so painful that it burned every time she tried to urinate. Mada started to hand the sheaf to Bill, but was intercepted by Mahfuzah. The girl studied the drawing and realized she was in a semi conscious state when most of the escape took place. She said to her mother, in her native tongue, "Thank you faithful mother, for saving me. We *will* live together always." Then, she handed the sheet to Bill who placed it face down on top of the others. Mahfuzah then tore a blank sheet off the pad, saying once again. "My story." She waited several minutes before she selected a very fine rolling ball pen, a Pilot Precise V5, a favorite of Bill's for meticulously recording in his little notebook, weigh station results, fuel costs, miles driven and so on. He was pleased she chose that particular pen to tell her story, oddly believing there was a connection between them, however ephemeral it might be.

Mahfuzah examined the tip, and put pen to paper. Drawing freehand but with the precision of a draughtsman using a T-square, she outlined a very small rectangular box in the exact center of the page no more than one and a quarter inch wide and three quarters of an inch in height. She put the pen down to examine her work. Satisfied, she picked up the pen again and wrote three words in English inside the box, handing it to Bill. The letters were so tiny; Bill needed to put on his reading glasses to see what Mahfuzah had written. He read the words out loud: "I Want Me".

Bill looked at Mahfuzah and was tempted to ask her the meaning behind the words, but the girl's body language indicated he would have to figure that out for himself.

Was she trapped inside a box, with no way out? Did she think of herself as insignificant? Or, that her world was so small? After painfully viewing Mada's very revealing pictorial narrative, he considered Mahfuzah's miniature output an enigma. When and how, Bill thought, will this young girl have a life that is worth living? That question may never be answered to his satisfaction, not knowing whether their lives would continue to be intertwined. Bill decided it was the right time to call his wife. He moved to the other end of the table to make the call. He took out his phone and began to dial but stopped. He needed to first anticipate Tricia's shock and bewilderment. He had better prepare answers to her poignant questions. Where are they from? Suppose they carry a disease? Do you want to start a countrywide epidemic? He wanted Tricia to meet them, to hear their story. Buy them some clothes. Let them have a warm bath and a soft bed to lie on. Maybe get them some necessary medical help, legal advice, opportunities for school and for work, then send them out. His mind was buzzing with many possible options. He did not have one satisfactory answer for what he knew Tricia would most likely ask. As best he could, without being able to verbally communicate with them, he might have to do some drawings of his own.

He returned to the other end of the table. He asked Mahfuzah a few simple questions to see how far it would get him as far as her understanding of the circumstances that drew the three of them together. She made believe she did not understand a word he was saying. Bill then tried another tactic. He made a simple drawing of his house with trees and a yard with a tall, fair- haired woman standing with open arms at the front door, two dogs at her side.

Bill felt like he was back in kindergarten but felt vindicated when both Mada and Mahfuzah smiled at his efforts. Most importantly, he was able to determine whether or not they believed they might have any kind of disease. He mentioned buzzwords like doctor, nurse, hospital, and did some simple drawings of beds and IV poles and whatever else came to mind. Mahfuzah shook her head and spoke to her mother in Arabic. Mada nodded affirmatively and took a dog-eared card out of her shirt pocket and handed it to Bill. It was a Medecin Sans Frontiers record card containing a history of the injections, including mumps and diphtheria, they both received at a refugee camp. He felt relieved. He pressed further about how they got into the United States but Mahfuzah only answered in pantomime how they crossed many wild rivers and snuck around border guards. Who helped them, he inquired. A friend was the only answer forthcoming. There never was an angel.

The storm had shifted east and north, leaving behind a sloppy road heading west but easily navigable in the Peterbilt 579. They would reach Clarion in three hours, based on the Weather Watch on the BIG STOP TV screens. The snowplows and sand trucks were busy at work.

Tricia was skeptical about her husband's sudden plunge into missionary work but expressed a willingness to hear it from him firsthand, before the ladies stepped foot into their home. Also, she was not happy Bill risked a thousand-dollar payday by aborting his trip to New England.

By using the storm as an excuse, he bought some time with his client, but lost a little luster off his one hundred percent dependable reputation. Although he promised to be back on the road in no more than a few days, he never before let bad weather stop him from his appointed rounds.

He would first drive to the depot to get the trailer unhitched, then park the truck under the canopy he had built on the side of his house. Tricia warned him over the phone that their curious neighbors might be watching through their blinds at the sight of two foreign, dark-skinned ladies wearing blue and white Keystone State sweatshirts. That scene would raise more than a few eyebrows, so she suggested that she meet them at the side entrance with a big blanket to shield their grand entrance into a brand new world. Let's do it, Tricia told him, displaying a rare sense of adventure.

Mada and Mahfuzah were not so sure they were ready to experience a totally new world. When the time came to enter the house, the two women held each other tightly as they slipped under the cover of a blanket held aloft by Bill and Tricia into the Clarion home. They both bowed deeply as they were greeted by Tricia, who herself performed an awkward curtsy in return. She escorted them to the *en suite* bedroom on the first floor usually reserved for her mother's visits.

Mada and Mahfuzah sat on the edge of the queen-size bed, holding hands. They did not budge an inch for the half hour Bill went through the drawings with Tricia, who immediately dismissed any reservations she had about offering assistance. She held back her tears once she pieced together their story and kicked into high efficiency mode. There was much to consider and much to do. She would take over from here she told Bill as he needed to get back on the road no later than tomorrow to deliver his payload. Obviously, they are here illegally so whomever the Reynolds contacted had to be close friends and trusted associates obligated to keep everything they heard in the strictest confidence. Tricia's mother would be excluded from the loop.

In her work as office administrator for a local insurance company, Tricia was proficient in keeping orderly files for the salespeople and for being the office go-to person capable of unclogging any jam that obstructed office procedures and protocol. She was the right person for this job.

Tricia put a pot of chicken soup on the stove and headed to the bedroom. Bill went upstairs to take a shower. He could not have been happier with his wife. If anyone could figure out where to go next and develop a step-by-step plan, it was she. As Tricia entered the bedroom, she smiled at the sight of the diminutive mother and daughter. How could that tiny woman carry her daughter through the woods after such a harrowing episode? It is not humanly possible, she thought.

Tricia knew instinctively that she had a lot to learn from this heroic woman, not the least of which was the uncharted limits of an indomitable human spirit. As they sat rigidly on the edge of the bed, and would not move, not knowing what they were supposed to do or how they were expected to behave, Tricia walked to the side of the bed and did a backwards free fall on the mattress, giving Mada and Mahfuzah quite a shake. Their little bodies popped up like kids on an Amazing Bouncy Castle Ride. Tricia produced another exaggerated fall onto the bed, which made them laugh. Tricia gestured to them that the bed is theirs.

Mada and Mahfuzah never slept on a bed, only on a straw mat or a cot in their hut and in the refugee camps. They were handed soap, shampoo, soft towels and washcloths by Tricia who showed them how to draw a deliciously warm bubble bath. Previously, they never took a bath in a tub, only in the river or occasionally a cold shower in the camp. Tricia, at least a head taller than Mada, gently put mother and daughter side by side so she could size them up for a guestimate on clothing sizes. That being done, she put Bill in charge of the soup and toast and drove to the nearby Goodwill store, scooping up pants, blouses, underwear, and shoes all from the children's section. She would buy them brand new clothing downtown when more time allowed.

The first call Tricia made on their behalf was to her good friend, Lynn, who worked as a Nurse Practitioner in a group medical practice three days a week and as a floater in a large general hospital the other two days. Mada and Mahfuzah need a physical examination. With giving Lynn only the barest of information, she inquired if she knew of a Muslim woman at the hospital who was conversant in Arabic and more importantly, that this woman be a person of uncompromised discretion. The woman could be a medical professional or a cleaning lady. It did not matter. She would be compensated for her trouble. Lynn agreed to help, would make the necessary inquiries and report back to Tricia once she had the desired information.

Tricia next called a close attorney friend she met through the insurance office and discreetly inquired if he could recommend a competent immigration lawyer. Tricia had the same concerns as Bill about Mahfuzah. Did she ever go to school? At what level was she, what grade? How could they enroll her in the local public school system? For the time being, they would get her a computer and download a dual Arabic/English language program. There was much to find out. But slow down. Draw up a list. One issue at a time. Keep it simple. They cannot be kept indoors indefinitely. They are not prisoners. Could Mada pass as a live-in cleaning lady without raising suspicions? Do not get stressed out.

Lynn showed up the next day and examined both Mada and Mahfuzah. She came with a trusted friend from the hospital, a Saudi woman, Hakimah, who worked as a clerk in the admissions office. Mada was more shy about the exam than her daughter, peremptorily knowing she had issues the nurse would most likely discover. When Lynn put on her gloves and mask, Mahfuzah asked her with a broad smile, "Medecin sans frontiers?"

Lynn answered her in English with Hakimah translating, "Yes, very much like them. We all feel privileged to help lovely people like you."

When Lynn discovered specific issues, she asked Hakimah to ask the women relevant questions, which needed to be discussed later. Lynn was very gentle with the women, but thorough in her examination. She was getting a disquieting idea of some of the trauma they experienced, just from the language their violated bodies communicated.

As Tricia met with Lynn and Hakimah in the kitchen, Mada and Mahfuzah remained behind in the bedroom. They took advantage of the free time and drew another hot bubble bath, now branded by them as the ultimate luxury.

"Thank you, Lynn," Tricia said, "I am so grateful you came so quickly. What do I need to know?"

"I'll have to toss HIPPA rules out the window because these are special circumstances," Lynn rationalized, looking for affirmation from Hakimah, who placed both hands over her mouth, "Mada especially needs to see one of our gynecologists. There are several lesions on the walls of her vagina. Possibly a fistula that was repaired in a hurry. That's my opinion, but any further diagnosis or treatment is beyond my skill set."

Hakimah added, "Mada told us she was raped by several men. When the last one was finished, she was dazed but definitely felt a different kind of hard object jammed inside of her, maybe a pipe, wood pole, or the barrel of a rifle. She is not sure. The doctors treated her at the camp. Whether they were finished or not, we don't know. Word spread around the camp that the host country planned to send them back to the place from which they fled. There was no home or village to return to. Everything was destroyed. The idea of future violence in that same country was unacceptable. Mada seized the opportunity to escape when it was offered to her."

"By whom?" Tricia asked.

"A volunteer, is all she'd say," Hakimah answered.

"What about Mahfuzah," Tricia asked, looking at both women, "will she be okay?"

Lynn and Hakimah looked at each other. Lynn answered the question, "At one point she went almost into a trance, and kept repeating three words, over and over again, rocking back and forth."

"What three words?" Tricia asked.

Hakimah spoke, "I want me. I want me. I want me."

Tricia took a mental health leave from work to spend the first week with her new houseguests. She had to get them settled. Fearing their presence would become public, she could not risk that they would innocently open the door when either she or Bill were not home.

Just like her husband, Tricia very quickly found herself getting very attached to both Mada and Mahfuzah.

She told Bill, "I'm all in on this". Fully aware how real the potential was concerning the risk of deportation, Tricia realized the women could not be kept hidden indefinitely even though they seemed quite happy taking hot baths, helping with the meals and cleaning, and learning more and more English on the computer every day. Getting way ahead of herself, Tricia imagined that she would take them to the hair salon, the farmer's market, and all the other everyday things western Pennsylvania women are accustomed to doing.

It was now late January. She and Bill met with the immigration attorney and learned about some of their options, which were somewhat vague yet precious few in number, especially since the women entered the country, 'without inspection', as the lawyer explained.

There was more of a realistic path for Mahfuzah since she was a minor, but Mada was at great risk. After the meeting in the lawyer's office, she regretted allowing them to play with the dogs in the back yard, just a few days earlier. The cocker spaniels, Sweetie, the mother and her son, Roughie, were affable canines and took to the mother and daughter after only a few sniffs. Sweetie was old and unable to keep up with the energetic Roughie who ran in and out of Mahfuzah's legs to her constant delight. When Sweetie ambled over to the corner of the yard, and started to scrape the ground with her front paw, Mahfuzah asked, "What is she doing?"

Tricia told her, matter-of-factly, "She is getting ready to do her business."

Mahfuzah, although learning English words on the computer, did not realize they were not always accompanied by nuanced, alternate meanings. She laughed out loud, saying, "Sweetie is in business!"

"No," Tricia explained, "that's just a way of saying she is getting ready to poop." She made a farting noise with her mouth that sent Mahfuzah running around the yard, laughing even louder, saying, "Poop. Poop. Poop," many times over.

They all had a good laugh. Mada and Mahfuzah learned several new words each day. They learned another funny word one night when Bill got home from a three-day trip. He brought them each a gift, giving Mada a new headscarf and presented a deck of cards to Mahfuzah, who had no idea what they were. They sat around a card table in the living room, enjoying a warm, cozy fire, as Bill tried to teach them a few simple games like Go Fish, Old Maid, and Gin Rummy. In the middle of one of the games, Tricia teased Bill and asked him if he was a cheat. Mada and Mahfuzah could not let go of that word and kept accusing the trucker of being a cheat. Bill laughed along until they all got giddy.

Several more weeks passed and it was the beginning of February. They ate breakfast together as one big, happy family. Bill was given a hearty safe travels by all three women as he prepared to leave on another assignment. Mahfuzah returned to the bedroom to learn more 'funny' English words.

Mada followed Tricia upstairs to help make the beds. Tricia dreaded this moment, not knowing how Mada would react to the information she learned from the immigration attorney. They sat down on one end of the bed, very close to each other. Instinctively, just like Bill on the first night he saw Mada in the bright interior light of his truck, Tricia noticed the vertical grayish black marks below Mada's eyes. She formed two fingers in a V-shape and gently traced them down her beautiful face, from just below the eyes, and unconsciously, even though it was a wildly different context, started singing almost in a whisper the Smokey Robinson song, "The Tracks of My Tears", "Although I may be laughing loud and hearty/Deep inside I'm blue/So take a good look at my face/You'll see my smile looks out of place/If you look closer, it's easy to trace/The tracks of my tears." Mada removed Tricia's hand and held it on her lap.

"Nice singing voice," Mada said.

"Thank you, Mada, can we ..."

"Talk?" Mada interrupted.

"Yes, I have some questions. Some information. Some things we need to decide."

"Me too," Mada said.

"Go ahead," Tricia said.

Mada, pointing to the bed, then the door, "Why two rooms?"

Tricia removed her hand from Mada's grasp, answering, "We don't sleep together anymore."

Mada did not ask why, but did want to know something else, so she asked her, "Hug?"

"You're asking me to hug you?" Tricia said.

Mada shook her head side to side, "No. Mahfuzah."

"You want me to hug Mahfuzah?"

"Later."

"You want me to hug your daughter later?" Tricia asked.

"Your daughter," Mada said, pointing right at Tricia and in return getting an even more pronounced question mark on her host's face.

Mada saw that she was not getting through and wished that Hakimah was there to translate even though this was all too personal and intimate for a third party to be present. She had to muddle through, as slow and as painful as it was, try not to weaken and avoid resorting to another exercise in kindergarten art like the night she executed those horrific drawings for Bill. They certainly would not bring about the desired outcome of what she needed to share. This conversation had to be one on one, face to face. No substitutes. Nothing else would do.

Mada held up her hands in the motion of stop or hold in a game of charades and decided a combination of her limited vocabulary and pantomime might do the trick. She ventured forth with her spur of the moment plan.

Tricia smiled and assured Mada that she appreciated the effort and would be very patient in trying to understand what she so desperately wanted to say.

"Mahfuzah and you," Mada started, pointing one hand at Tricia's head and with her other hand, touched Tricia's chest near her heart.

"You want to know if I love Mahfuzah with my head and my heart? Is that what you're asking me?"

Mada nodded her approval. Emboldened, she wanted to take the next step quickly so Tricia would understand that everything she is trying to say is bound by intimate and inextricable connections. Mada cradled her arms as if she was grasping somebody or some thing, "Hug Mahfuzah."

"I need to love Mahfuzah with my heart and mind AND my body. She needs physical contact, needs to know she is loved with hugs."

At that, Mada pursed her lips, to which Tricia won the charade game by saying, "Love her with hugs and kisses."

Mada nodded enthusiastically.

Sensing only what two women from entirely different worlds, literally and figuratively, could instinctively know about each other, Tricia began to tear up. Mada rushed over to the dresser and put the box of tissues between them. They would both have a good cry if this game of charades had a successful outcome.

Wanting to continue quickly, and not lose momentum, Mada laid it all out so they would each understand the other, "Me. Doctor" she said, "Get caught. Mahfuzah. School, get caught."

Tricia realized in that moment, that Mada, not knowing about attorneys, the law or the way things are done in this country, saved her the trouble by raising the exact subject they needed to talk about.

Mada took a deep breath, placed one hand on her heart, and her other on Tricia's heart, "You mother now."

There was a long period of silence before Mada said, without reservation, "I go."

Immediately, Tricia thought of the scenarios that the immigration lawyer spelled out. The first step would be to obtain legal custody of Mahfuzah. Then, log in two years of legal physical custody. Since she entered the country without inspection, probably with the help of a smuggler, there would be required a filing of a visa petition with the United States Citizenship and Immigration Services. Once that petition is approved, assuming it would be, the next step would be going through the green card process. Even though adopting an undocumented immigrant can be complicated, if Mahfuzah is considered an orphan less than sixteen years of age, then there are some positive alternative paths that can lead to legal adoption.

Without her biological mother, Mahfuzah would indeed be an orphan and thereby make the path to adoption all the more feasible. Mada was right. All it would take is one nosy neighbor to spread the word, one curious conversation with a friend whose niece happens to be married to an immigrations officer. One innocent trip to the supermarket, one casual walk around the block with the dogs. Deportation. A return ticket to where the devil reigns supreme, where neither country wants you or your daughter.

"You cannot go, Mada," Tricia implored, "If Bill and I have to hide you in the basement, or move to another country, we will. This will destroy Mahfuzah."

Mada held up four fingers and counted down on them, "Sick. Die. Caught. Gone."

Tricia protested, "Lynn can get a doctor to come to our house. There are medicines, procedures."

"I tell Mahfuzah tonight" Mada said with finality.

Tricia called Bill while he was on the road. He managed to hear the story through her sobbing. He said he'd drive through the night to be home before morning.

That night, as Bill guzzled a giant black coffee as he drove, Tricia knew she would not sleep one minute.

Together in bed, mother and daughter remembered the lost loved ones, as they did every night before going to sleep:

"Raheel." "Father." "Arfan." "Brother "Muhammad." "Baby brother."

After a few more incantations, Mada spoke in Arabic with her daughter and told her that she needed to go away for a while. Soon.

With the heartfelt innocence of a child yet with the mature wisdom of an adult who has experienced the equivalent of ten difficult lifetimes, she asked, "Will you come back to me, mother?"

"Yes, if I am able."

"When will you go?"

"Some day, I will just disappear."

"I cannot live without you."

"Yes you can. You *will* live in freedom. Some day, you will bear beautiful children of your own."

"I will name the boys Arfan and Muhammad. And the girl will be named Mada."

"Tricia will be your next mother. Will you love her?"

"Does she love me?"

"She loves you with her heart and mind and hugs and kisses, just like I do."

"Will you love Bill?" Mahfuzah did not answer. Mada suggested, "He is funny."

"Yes, he is funny but he is not like father."

"No. He is not. But he is *not* like those soldiers. He would have killed those men who violated you."

"I will try to love him, mother."

"Also, you will one day meet a man who might not be like your father or funny like Bill, but he will be kind and gentle and will respect you and protect you."

Bill arrived home several hours before sunrise. Tricia was waiting for him in the living room. No words were spoken between them as they ascended the stairs. Bill entered his bedroom. He took off his shirt, pants and socks and threw them in a pile on the floor. Moments later, Tricia slipped under the covers with her husband and they slept together until mid morning.

When they came downstairs, Mada and Mahfuzah had breakfast waiting for them. When Mada would later go upstairs to make the beds, she was pleased to find out that Bill and Tricia had a reunion.

Ten days later Mada disappeared. She slipped out of the house in the middle of the night, when Mahfuzah was in a deep sleep. She left behind on Mahfuzah's night table one of the drawings Bill had returned to her. It was the one Mahfuzah drew, of the tiny rectangular box with the three words "I Want Me" written inside. Mada added four more boxes beneath the original one:

"Your mother wants you."
"Your next mother wants you."
"Bill wants you."
"The whole world wants you."

When Mahfuzah awoke. She read her mother's note, folded it, and placed it in the top drawer of the night table. She stayed in bed the entire day, not changing out of her pajamas. Mahfuzah also failed to come outside her room for breakfast, lunch or dinner. Around nine p.m. Tricia knocked on her door and asked if she could enter.

Mahfuzah said yes. Tricia opened the door. The lights were not on but with the ambient light emanating from the streetlamp outside, she saw the outline of Mahfuzah's small body, appearing even smaller this night, diminished by the loss of her mother. The child froze in place, staring at a fixed point on the ceiling as she had done all day.

Tricia sat in the armchair, watching her. After ten minutes she asked if she could lie down next to her, just for a little while. Mahfuzah said it was okay to do so. Tricia lay there for a quarter hour without a word being spoken, then decided to whisper softly,

"Raheel." Silence.

"Arfan." Silence.

"Muhammad." Silence.

Tricia waited a few moments more, speaking in a quiet voice, tried again, "Raheel."

Tricia waited longer this time before Mahfuzah's small voice responded, "My father."

"Arfan," Tricia said reverently.

More quickly than before, Mahfuzah echoed. "Arfan! My brother!"

"Muhammad," Tricia said.

"My baby brother!" said Mahfuzah.

Then, without waiting, Tricia spoke boldly, "Mada."

"Mother. My mother!" Mahfuzah screamed.

They each repeated the refrain over and over again until they were both exhausted. Tricia sat up in the bed. Mahfuzah came close to her, then allowed her body to limply fill the crevice created by Tricia's arms and body. Tricia hugged her and kissed her, and stroked her hair until she fell asleep. Tricia stayed with her throughout the night.

THE FARM

He was all eyes and twitching fingers in the video. He came to rob the house through the basement window. Instead, he got trapped in the medieval stockade our engineers constructed. It was definitely a 'smile, you're on Candid Camera' moment but not one he would ever want to reminisce about. The sudden blast of the flash from inside a completely dark basement created quite a stunning yearbook photo. It highlighted his best features: neglected teeth and gums; unwashed and uncombed hair; and a significant hole in his nose, where a ring once was but now had the circumference of a third nostril. We systematically catalog these photos and videos in the unlikely event that our new captives insist on a trial. Exhibit A and exhibit B are usually quite damning. Besides, we would never agree to a jury trial as the only people our captives (we don't call them prisoners) ever meet are already members of The Society.

We watched this one particular young man for one whole week. He snooped around the house for a few days, kind of nonchalantly at first. Then, after he built up his confidence, he'd pass by the house, walk to the end of the block, and jot down some notes in his little pad. A student, we thought. How admirable. As we awaited the day he would make his bold decisive move, and illegally enter an unsuspecting person's house, we weren't one hundred percent sure our latest contraption would work. Prior to the development of this device, all we had was a fast-closing window. No one ever escaped from the window but one unfortunate would-be criminal did sustain a serious neck injury. That incident also inconvenienced us as we had to procure discreet medical help for him before we transported him to The Farm. In addition, he had to wear a neck brace for two months, which rendered him useless in terms of doing his share of the work on The Farm.

This new device, however, works exceptionally well. It exhibits a certain fluid movement combined with a patented 'smart contour' feature. One part comes up and the other comes down together in the blink of an eye. It has the look of a casement window but the photo and heat sensors capture the head and the wrists in an iron-tight grip. Perfect! We plan to use it on all the miscreants we catch in the future.

Medieval stockades were often used to break and humiliate a person because those locked inside with head and hands dangling faced public humiliation as their punishment. That was centuries ago. We take a more humane approach in this device's implementation. Also, we're not too keen on anyone outside of The Society becoming the least bit aware of our existence and our mission so we're basically publicity shy to put it mildly.

Let me make this perfectly clear from the outset. The criminals we summarily remove from decent society will never become members of our *Society*. We are fully aware of all the statistics on recidivism. We are not some New Age altruistic group of psychologists who think we now have the answer to rehabilitating hardened criminals and reintroducing them back into the civilized world. We are not interested in the implementation of some doctoral candidate's thesis that proposes to save the world because the sociologist found enough supportive statistical data on the internet and in the hallowed confines of the Columbia University Graduate School Library. Our only interest is to remove these lowlifes from the streets and put them to work on The Farm. We unashamedly profit from their labor. Their parents, if they happen to have any, rarely manage to stay sober long enough to realize the little darlings are even missing.

This brings us to the next issue of the strict procedures we follow as to not humiliate these captives any more than is necessary. After we photograph and videograph the criminal in the act, one of our members goes outside, pulls the pants down on this poor unfortunate and gives him a little sleepy-bye injection in his buttocks. In the rare event of catching a female thief in the act, we always follow protocol and employ a like gender member of our Society to apply the injection.

Now that we have our little charge under control and fast asleep in la la land, we secure him for the four-hour ride in the back of the van, and keep him under constant guard for the whole trip. We assume our little weasel's name is Charlie from the sketchy identity we obtained from his wallet. There's always the chance that the ID inside the wallet belongs to someone he robbed. Our catch is about 5'7", Caucasian, with a fair amount of artless tattoos on his arms and back. As we stated earlier, he's in serious need of major dental care but that is not our concern. Our objective is to get him upstate in about four hours and release him on the property just prior to his rude awakening. It is not our custom to visually record this segment of our activities but I wouldn't be surprised if Charlie, groggy from the anesthesia and all alone in a wide open field, bearing his most recent memory of the instantaneous locking in of his neck and wrists and having been blasted with our powerful camera flash, then absorbing a pinprick in his bottom cheeks, might express some look of bewilderment when he arises on all fours to gaze upon an open field with little to hope for and much less to see.

Charlie woke up with his nose pressed against the wet grass. It was early in the morning. The air was fresh and clean, as the thunderstorm in the middle of the night broke the oppressive summer heat as the skies poured down some necessary rain. This part of the terrain does not look like a farm. It is an enormous open field, green grass and clover as far as the eye can see. Charlie was dropped off on the highest elevation of the land, so it would be impossible for him to see that a high barbed-wire fence occupied the entire perimeter of the field, with the exception of the large three-story house on the extreme northern end. We watched him through our field glasses as he got up and staggered a few steps. He was still a little wobbly from the anesthesia. He patted his pockets, checking for his cell phone and wallet most likely, but we had carefully removed all items from his clothing. This was no Fresh Air Fund summer camp for inner city kids but chances are Charlie has never before seen such a wide expanse of green. It would do him well to take a deep breath and soak in the atmosphere. Even though we don't call them sentences, he would most likely be with us for quite some time.

Charlie did a 360-degree turn and, like most of our captives, opted to head in the direction of the house. It took a good twenty minutes for him to get close to the front door. By now he was probably able to see the perimeter fence, although the house looked like it had an escape route on either side. Of course, that was not the case. When we designed The Farm, we obscured the fence on either side of the house with rows of trees and brush. Our favorites are the tall boxwood hedges, which give off a nice country aroma, mixed in with a lovely variety of blue spruces and scotch pines. They are absolutely beautiful in every season, especially in winter when the heavy snows cause the branches to droop like a casually worn necklace.

The Dutch Colonial house was built in 1923, designed by the Dross Horton architectural firm. The house had the typical broad gambrel shape with flared eaves extending over the porches. The DH firm was known for using only the best building materials for all of their developments but we adapted the large house many times over to suit our very specialized needs. Behind the house was another large parcel of land, not quite as big as the one in front, and certainly not as open. It was well fortified all around and was heavily landscaped with a series of outbuildings and sheds where our captives slept and where they worked for our profit and for their eventual freedom. Obviously, we are not commissioned by any government agency to turn out license plates or anything of that nature. Also, The Farm is not a traditional farm in the sense that there are no animals about, other than a pet parakeet and a few cats. No pigs or cows or horses are anywhere to be seen. No crops are grown anywhere on the land either. No corn, lettuce, not even a single tomato will ever grow out of the ground at The Farm.

By force of habit, Charlie surveyed each double hung sash window along the front of the house. He peered inside but ultimately decided to make use of the front door. He gave the antique lion's head knocker a few good raps and waited. The door was opened to him by Anna. She is our official greeter. We're not sure of her exact age and she's a little bit fuzzy about it herself. Our best guess is that she is in her early eighties. She can't be much taller than 4'11" and is a little bent over with age. However, she has the brightest personality, sparkling almost. We rarely ever see her in a cranky mood. Her white hair and hazel eyes invite the most pleasant reception from everyone she meets. A real professional grandmotherly type. Warm and loving but somewhat forgetful. She heard the knock and opened the door immediately, not even inquiring who was on the other side. She motioned with her delicate and frail right hand for Charlie to step into the grand entrance, which he did without wiping his dirty sneakers on the small rug, put there for that purpose.

Anna started the conversation, in a voice that could only be considered angelic, with soft, lilting, almost musical tones: "Can I offer you something to drink? Some tea or juice. Maybe you're hungry. I"ll make you a sandwich. Tuna fish? Egg salad?"

As she spoke, Charlie looked all around, at the high ceiling, and the two brick fireplaces in the living room off to the right. After he took it all in, he faced the tiny grandmother and said,

"Where the fuck am I?"

Unfazed by his rude manner, Anna answered him, "In my house. Well, I don't actually own it. But I do live here. I've lived here for quite some time."

"I know it's a house lady. I want to know what fucking town I'm in. Where the fuck am I?"

"Upstate. This house is upstate."

Lacking patience as a general rule, Charlie raised his voice a notch, "What state lady? Just answer my fucking question, will you."

"Why, the state I grew up in. I've lived here most of my life." At that, Charlie sat down in the corner, by the door, and rested one elbow on the ceramic umbrella stand. He held his head in his free hand, still feeling the after effects of the drug. After a moment, he asked, "Do you have a phone I could use?"

"I don't think so. I never saw one here. That's a bit odd, now that I think of it. My daughter writes to me. And sometimes she visits. She took me to the podiatrist last week. I had a terrible pain in my foot."

Charlie looked up at her and said, "Do you live here by yourself?"

"Oh God, no. A lot of people live here. Men and women. Boys and girls. Not little boys and girls. Children just about your age. Some a little older. Some younger."

"Is there someone else here I could speak to? Or, is there another house around?"

"Are you sure you won't eat something? You look so tired. Maybe you want to rest for a bit. Let me see if one of the beds upstairs is made up." Anna turned toward the staircase but then stopped and faced Charlie, "Did you hear that?"

"What? Hear what?"

"The bird. The bird in the cage in the living room. My little paraclete."

"Parakeet!" Charlie corrected her.

"You know. You can take care of him. That can be your job. First time guests usually get to take care of my Paraclete. Go in and visit with him. At least I think it's a him although it might be a her. They say it's the color of the beak that gives the gender away. But I think we need to take a sample of its blood, just to make sure. What do you think? What's your name? You look so familiar. Were you ever here before?"

Charlie looked at her and did not answer. Anna headed upstairs. Charlie stood up and tried to open the front door. It wouldn't budge. He grabbed the knob with both hands and pulled it so hard that it came completely out of the door, causing him to fall backwards on his rump. He rushed into the living room and tried to open the windows but all of them were sealed shut. He tried to break the glass with the brass doorknob but found out after a few tries that the windows must have been made out of a substance stronger than glass. He threw the knob to the floor and picked up a heavy bronze sculpture of a cowboy on horseback and was just about to throw it through the surface when a man's hand grabbed his wrist from behind.

The man removed the sculpture from Charlie's grip and pushed him into a chair near the fireplace.

"This is a very expensive sculpture by Remington. A first bronze casting. You almost damaged it. I can see you don't have much appreciation for art," the man said, as he stood over Charlie, still dazed from his encounter with Anna. Maybe now he could get some straight answers.

"Listen mister, I just want to get the fuck out of here. The door's locked. The windows are shut. Just show me the way out and I won't be any trouble to anyone."

"Don't you want something to eat or drink before you go?" the man asked. Charlie tried to stand up but the man's imposing physical presence did not allow him to move in any direction.

"Excuse me, do you mind if I stand up?" Charlie asked.

"Oh, you do have manners, then. No. You can't stand up. Stay right where you are. I need to interview you for a few minutes and then I'll show you what routines you need to follow in order to properly take care of Anna's Paraclete."

"Who are you? What is this place? You can't hold me here. Kidnapping's against the law. I'll tell the police exactly what you're doing."

The man backed away from the chair and sat down opposite Charlie. He pulled a clipboard out of the side table drawer. It had a foolscap pad and a pencil tethered to it. "How are going to do that?" the man asked.

"Do what!" Charlie shot back, anxious about what to do or say next.

"You just said something about the law and the police. Tell me what your plan is. Tell me exactly how you're going to contact the police and what it is that you're going to tell them. The nearest station is miles from here and you wouldn't have any way of knowing which direction to go."

Charlie sank back in the chair. As open and warm as this living room was that he presently occupied, Charlie started to sense that he was in deep trouble. The walls, hung with tapestries and gilded frame paintings and other bric-a-brac he had only seen in magazine ads, started to close in on him. He had no weapon and he knew just from looking at the man with the clipboard that he couldn't overpower him. Although his mind was a lot clearer now than it was an hour earlier, he felt nauseous and started to sweat. "Where am I?" he asked politely.

"You're in a house on The Farm located upstate. The Farm is run by members of The Society. I am here to give you an introduction to how things are done around here. It's like an orientation."

"Am I a prisoner?" Charlie wanted to know.

"We don't use that term around here."

"Then, why can't I go?" Charlie pleaded, his voice cracking a little bit.

"We'll talk all about that later. First, you need to answer a few questions," with that, the man crossed his legs and rested the clipboard on his knee, ready to take down everything Charlie said, "can you tell me the last thing you remember before you arrived at The Farm?"

"I was playing basketball with my friends."

"Day or night?"

"Day or night what?"

"Were you playing basketball during the day or at night."

"Listen. I don't have to answer this shit. Just let me out of here before I ..."

"Before you what?" the man asked calmly.

"I'll give you money. Just let me out of here."

"The Society does not accept bribes. We are a self-funding and self-insured organization. Besides, you only had $231 in your wallet. How much were you planning on giving us, anyway?"

"Hey, you stole my wallet!"

"We took your wallet, cell phone, and keys. We threw away the breath mints. They were stale. By the way, you should consider using sugarless mints. They're better for your teeth. You'll get everything back whenever you leave."

"I have a lot of money. Thousands. I got it back home. I just got to get back home and I'll give you everything I have. Just let me out of here. You can come with me. I'll turn it all over to you. No questions asked. I swear to God. I'll never tell anybody I was here."

"How did you accumulate thousands? You seem so young to have *thousands*."

"Work. I got it from work and saved it up. I swear mister, you can have it all."

"What kind of work do you do?" the man asked, prepared to write down Charlie's answer, and then said, "You don't have to answer that. You'll make plenty for us here over the years."

"Years? I need a lawyer," Charlie screamed.

A second man came into the room from the kitchen area, walked over to Charlie and extended his hand to greet him. "Hello Charlie, my name is Bill. I'm an attorney." Bill then sat down in a chair alongside of the man conducting the interview. "George," he said, "I think it's time we tell Charlie what it is that we do here, what's expected of him short term and long term, and then show him to his living quarters. After all, he's had a long day already."

"Fair enough," George said, placing the clipboard down on top of the table, "why don't you explain everything to him."

Bill looked directly at Charlie and in a kind, soft voice, said, "Before I give my little speech, do you have any questions you want to ask us?"

Feeling for the first time the slightest bit of encouragement since the moment he came through the front door, Charlie looked up at the attorney and said, "Just two questions. Where am I and when can I leave?"

Bill leaned forward, staring directly into the young man's eyes, speaking in the same reassuring tone, "You're upstate on The Farm. Exactly when you'll be permitted to leave all depends on how good a worker you are." The momentary flight of hope Charlie rode on, suddenly crashed to the wood plank floor.

The interview went about as well as all the previous interviews conducted by George on behalf of The Society. It was explained to Charlie that he had an impressive choice of trades he could learn while a resident on The Farm. He could learn photography or pottery making or rug weaving and knitting, plus several others. Whatever products or clothing made on The Farm were sold to the general public through auction sites on the internet. It is a very profitable business venture in that the labor costs are reduced to zero, with the exception of the cost of housing and meals. All proceeds go into The Society's General Fund.

Charlie worked in the shipping department for a few months but never saw a label or address stamp placed on the packages that would reveal the location of The Farm. Packages were prepared in one shed and then put on a shelf in another. A member of The Society coded them. They were all shipped the next day. Charlie would have to live with the notion of being 'upstate 'a while longer.

Charlie befriended a few other males in his shed and it did not take long for him to realize that he and his new buddies were all involved in the same 'business 'back home. One night, the conversation got around to making plans for an escape. One of the boys told Charlie about a door in the main house which leads to an underground tunnel. One of the shed mates escaped six months earlier and was never heard from again. Everyone assumed that he made a successful getaway. After that brazen adventure, the members of The Society held a meeting of the entire camp. The captives were warned that any thought of escape should be erased from their minds. There were real dangers connected to carrying out such a plan. They made it sound like a campfire ghost story.

Thinking that he was losing his mind anyway, Charlie plotted his escape. In the middle of the night some weeks later, he found his way into the main house and opened the door leading to the tunnel. He felt a little uncomfortable at first because it all seemed too easy. Why hadn't others tried this same route? Was it the fear of the unknown?

The only existence any of them knew was the world of the unknown. Upstate. The Farm. The Society. Charlie had enough of that and yearned for his freedom. He didn't want to be a rug weaver, or a potter or any other kind of idiotic tradesman. He wanted out and out he went, through the door, down the stairs and into the unlit tunnel.

Charlie walked for hours in total darkness, feeling his way around corners, never losing hope. What drove his spirit and kept him pushing, pushing toward freedom, was the all-consuming desire for revenge. He'd get some of his boys back home and turn the tables around on the members of The Society. He'd tie them up and hold a clipboard on his lap and interrogate them. His heart was being hardened and he thrilled to the idea of burning the place down to the ground after torturing them sufficiently, even the little white-haired old lady.

He had no idea how long he had been walking and crawling in this damp place. He needed to rest for a few moments before he could go any further. He sat down on the damp ground and fell asleep in a seated position. He had no idea of how long he slept but when he awakened his heart jumped. What looked like a thin shaft of light came creeping around the next corner – the next corner he scrambled to. The light grew in intensity and soon its luminescence filled more and more of the space in the tunnel. Charlie finally reached a crude staircase made of haphazardly placed stones. He scrambled to the top and kissed the ground and even ate some of the grass in celebration. This was his first taste of delicious, dirty freedom. He then saw cars whizzing by on the road some thirty yards distant. He ran to the edge of the road and saw a police car on the other side, hidden in a natural alcove with a policeman at the steering wheel, pointing a radar gun at the oncoming traffic.

Charlie never in his life thought he would take pleasure in the sight of a police officer. But he did. He could have kissed him. He ran up to the squad car and breathlessly explained the ordeal he was forced to live through. The police officer took an immediate interest in him and told him to get in the front seat so they could drive to headquarters and get to the bottom of all of this. While they were riding on the winding country road, the police officer asked, "Where is this house? What did it look like?"

"It's a huge house. Three stories. It had a roof that looks like a big hat," Charlie told him, anxious for the day when these people would pay for their crime. The police officer told Charlie that there are a lot of houses in the county that fit that description.

"County?" Charlie thought to himself, "I'm going to finally find out where I've been held prisoner." But first, he had to help the officer pinpoint this particular house. "There's a huge wide-open field in front of the house. It's got to be acres and acres wide and long," he said, then offered the clincher, "and behind the house are a bunch of sheds and rectangular shacks."

The officer said, "Okay. I think I know that place. Does a little old lady with white hair live there by any chance? A woman who goes by the name of Anna?"

"Yes!" Charlie yelled, almost busting loose from his seat.

The officer pulled into a parking space in front of a small wooden building bearing a sign: "Troop K Barracks". They walked together into the front office. Charlie sat down as the police officer handed him an ice cold bottle of water. The officer removed his hat and opened up the PC on his desk. He manipulated a few buttons and up on the screen came a Google Maps overhead view of The Farm.

"That's it! That's where those nuts kept me prisoner!"

"Okay. Settle down. If what you told me is true, there are a lot of laws being broken here." After a few moments, another police officer walked into the office. He carried some sizeable object by the metal handle and placed it on the other officer's desk. It stood about three feet high and was covered in burlap. As the officer started to remove the covering, Charlie began to realize what was contained inside. He immediately eyed the door, to see if he could make a break for it but held his ground, deciding it was too dangerous, keenly observing the pistols on the officer's belts. He could no longer tell the difference between illusion and reality. As the cover was about halfway up the cage, the first officer asked the other, "Is that Anna's paraclete?"

"Yes," the second officer said, "we just found out from the vet that she's a girl."

"Anna will like that. She always wanted to know. Now, she'll know for sure." Then, in the next moment, the officer spoke directly to Charlie, "so, young man, what else do you have to say for yourself."

Charlie's whole upper body slumped over, weakened to the point of ultimate defeat. He started to weep and through the sobs, with fluids spritzing uncontrollably out of his mouth, nose and eyes, he managed to confess to the officers, "I swear to God, I'll never steal another thing in my life. I swear it!" The second officer patted him on the back and spoke reassuringly, "That's a good start, Charlie. That's a damn good start."

Finally, the phone rang and it was Anna on the other end. The first officer said to his comrade in blue, "She wants us to bring her Paraclete back right now. She misses him ... I mean her.

THE COMPOST KING

"By the way, you might not guess it by his appearance, but he is a very deep thinker. Very often, he attacks a problem from an oblique angle so to speak, one that you or I might not even consider. He has a different kind of brain I have found. As unattractive as he is physically, he makes up for it with the beauty of his brain. Do you know that some cruel people call him hideous, odious, repulsive, right to his face. And other very unkind words, as if he did not have feelings like everyone else. As if a person's outward beauty is limited to his appearance and not his brain or his spirit. You know, when I least expect it, John comes up with a solution to a problem and, voila, the problem disappears. Remarkable. By the way, I'll mention to him the next time he's in town that you would like to have a sit-down with him. He'd be delighted that you've taken an interest in getting to know him better. And, might I add that a beautiful, intelligent woman like yourself will be enriched by the exchange. As he will also be learning something he did not know. He reads everything he can get his hands on. Nothing frivolous or superficial, mind you. No. His reading preference is for deep and sometimes dark literature. Well, let me clarify what I mean by literature, as far as he is concerned. I mean I'm sure he's read all of Charles Dickens' books, as well as American authors like Hawthorne and Melville, as well as the theatrical works of Shakespeare, and so on. I believe he once told me that he read all of the heady works written by the Greek polemicists. Yet overall, his taste tends more toward non-fiction, not made-up stuff or myths, but actual scholarly works on very obscure and arcane subjects. Mr. John Aubrey has such a depth of knowledge that will exhilarate you when you meet together in a more meaningful way. I will never be so presumptive to say or even suggest what you could offer to the conversation because I know there's much more to you than meets the eye. My God, just telling him about your passage to America on a coffin ship will make him fawn all over you. I just hope, Peggy. I truly hope, that you find satisfaction in your work here. That it doesn't bore you or make you feel unchallenged."

The well-meaning woman only asked Mr. Flaherty about her co-worker, John Aubrey, because she had no idea what he did for Flaherty's Lower East Side real estate enterprise. She left the boss's office with less information than when she entered and had no interest of any kind to interact socially with the Barbadian Aubrey.

Moments after Peggy left by the front door, Aubrey came through the trap door that accessed underground conduits connecting several of Flaherty's buildings. Matthew V. Flaherty's public identity revolved around his double role as U.S Congressman representing the 5th Ward and as a Tammany Hall big shot. Both of those responsibilities contributed greatly to the success of his real estate/construction business. The seed money for acquisition and construction came in part from the discretionary distribution of pushcart vendor and building permits. The fees for the privilege of selling wares and building tenements for Lower East Side immigrants were modest but were handsomely supplemented with aggressive bidding for those rights, for better or worse, controlled by the machinations of Tammany Hall.

For lack of a better job title, John Aubrey was Jack-Of-All-Trades and more in terms of assuring that Flaherty got the most votes on Election Day as well as the actualization of problem-free tenement construction. Any barriers to those goals were removed by Aubrey and his crew. The very nature of his work demanded he remain in the shadows.

The latest issue that came to Aubrey's attention was the obstacle presented by an ambitious Building Inspector named Horace Champlin, who slapped a heavy fine along with a Stop Order on one of Flaherty's alley huts he was in the process of building between two of his tenements. Flaherty's name was never associated with his business enterprises so Mr. Champlin knew nothing other than the name of the dummy corporation attempting to build an illegal windowless structure for a poor Irish immigrant and his family.

Aubrey sat in front of Flaherty's desk and studied the papers for a few minutes. He handed them back to his boss and said, "May I add a few more details about the mixture we'll be utilizing for this assignment?"

"Go right ahead, Mr. Aubrey."

"For this particular job I would like to add the hard spines of lettuce, and the prickly leaves of pineapple. Add a little broccoli wood too and broken eggshells - after the eggs are already scrambled. This will make an irresistible and highly compostable mix, I must say."

"You know your business, Mr. Aubrey. I would be the last person to question your choices. We just need a successful harvest," Flaherty said.

"Indeed. I need to make a special request, however." Mr. Aubrey said.

"And that is?"

"As you know, I am not the best record keeper. Paperwork just makes me daft. Although I admit it is a weakness of mine, I have devised a codified filing system that at long last works for me."

"And that is?" Mr. Flaherty said, delighting in this encounter.

"Well, the subject's initials are 'H' and 'C'. Therefore, I would like your permission to mark the crate Honeymelon Cabbage, if that meets with your approval."

"It does. It certainly does. Makes perfect sense. Go right ahead. Is the crew in town?"

"Yes sir. Ready, able and willing they are. I had quite a bit of trouble getting them out."

"Why is that?" Mr. Flaherty asked.

"They were quite eager to get out of Barbados but they kept making trouble down there. Beating up guards. Biting off ears. That kind of thing. I'm afraid I ran a bit over budget in tagging the authorities – the ones I know who've run up a few extra household bills. I found out who they were and worked with them. I don't want to bore you but you might see some extra charges in my expense account. However, I think the island is glad to be rid of our boys."

"I trust you John, Don't worry about that. What's more troubling and dearer is to hold up construction. We were just cruising along getting things built and then ..."

"Oh, you don't have to explain. I understand but if you'll permit me ..."

"Yes?" Mr. Flaherty said, curious.

"I would like to use this same crew for another assignment following this one. This way, the economics of the whole thing will even out over time. A form of amortization if you will."

"Tell me about it," Flaherty said.

"You have an re-election coming up, am I correct on that score?"

"Yes."

"I was not at all happy with the crew that worked the last election."

"The final vote was very close I seem to remember. Kept me up a few nights I have to admit," Flaherty said.

"That won't happen this time, I can assure you," Mr. Aubrey proudly stated, "these workers are ... how should I say it ... especially gifted. The composting work is not stimulating enough for them. They do it well but I have a strong feeling they will excel at the voting booth."

"Tell me more," said Flaherty, "By the way I worked out a truce with the *Musk Rats* gang. They won't prevent anyone from voting for me this time. Their boss actually apologized to me, explaining it was all a misunderstanding last time around."

John Aubrey laughed and said, "Oh, then we only have eight other gangs to contend with. Not to worry. I doubt they will play rough with your constituents in support of your opponent. We plan to keep a clear path open at the polls. With the men I have," Aubrey said as he pulled his chair closer to Flaherty's desk and lowered his voice, "They are even uglier than I am," he chortled, "As soon as I let them out of their cages one can see how truly grotesque they are. Yet somehow, in some strange way, *beautiful* in their disfigurations. The Almighty has blessed them with such strength. They just love to break backs with their bare hands, the only tools they need to assert a certain authority upon the audience. Yet given a different kind of tool, they will be even more adept. A sharp knife, for example. They know how to twist it as if it were a scalpel inside the body of a patient, expertly maneuvering the razor-sharp blade as if they were physiology students at Columbia Medical School. Their approach, of course, is neither academic or clinical. I don't boast they have the capacity for that. But they know instinctively all the normal functions of the body organs and how they perform in the whole drama of supporting one's willingness to live. When they twist the knife into one of those ruffians trying to thwart a legal election ... yours, in fact, the knife knows exactly what vital organ or vein it is penetrating. I hesitate to introduce them to you. Terribly difficult to look at, Mr. Flaherty. What's different about their approach, refined over the years under much harsher conditions in the islands when they themselves were abused with chains and clubs, and all sorts of other cruel instruments, only served to toughen them up."

Aubrey took a handkerchief out of his back pocket and wiped his brow. As he opened his mouth preparing to speak, one side of his lower lip drooped so that a drool of spittal flowed slowly over his crooked lip, and rode down his chin. He did not wipe it away immediately as that part of his face had become desensitized, the result of being cut during a vicious knife fight years earlier. This involuntary release was especially active whenever he became passionately animated talking about a favorite topic, "When I unleash them into a pile of brutes," he continued, "They won't start banging heads like other gang members, your *Cherry Street Rotter* boys will first blend into the crowd of humanity, unseen except for their repugnant physical appearance – but I will disguise them appropriately with floppy wide brim hats and long, nondescript cloaks. With special training, they will circulate amongst the rabble and root out the villains, not always so obvious even though they lack all subtlety and nuance of movement – ultimately they won't be hard to spot – anyhow, basically after the crowd clears, one will see a gathering of considerable lumps of dead meat scattered about on the grounds. Any of them still alive I'm afraid will be writhing in pain and will expire soon thereafter. Others might make it back home to tell their mothers how poorly they were bullied at school. You will get re-elected, Mr. Flaherty. I would put everything I own on that single bet."

Flaherty came around to John Aubrey's side and put his arm around the man's broad, rounded shoulders, "Thank you John. I can see that was a profitable recruitment junket for you ... for us. Don't worry about the additional expenses related to the trip. That should never be your worry. That is mine." Flaherty pulled a chair closer to his employee and sat down next to him. Looking at him directly, he said, "Are you lonely where you are now, John? Did you ever consider finding a woman to look after you? For companionship?"

John Aubrey straightened up in his chair as best he could and said, "Oh, I would never do that to a woman. I am not *that* cruel. Imagine her fright when she wakes up one morning from a troubling dream and the first thing she looks at is a true nightmare with all my hideous, odious, reddened, protruding facial scars from the top of my head through the eye socket right down to my twisted mouth that were never properly stitched. I have no delusions about my appearance, Mr. Flaherty. Like any man I lust after women but I get my jollies off in the fruit and vegetable business," with that said Aubrey let out with a jocular roar, joined by Flaherty who gave him another pat on his abnormally curved back.

"So, you're satisfied, are you," Flaherty asked, "With a little room, just a bed and a candle, surrounded by your books?"

"Ah, yes," Aubrey said, lighting up his disfigured eyes, "They are sufficient for me."

"What new subject matter is nudging its way into that big brain of yours now?" Flaherty said.

"If you would permit me ..."

"But of course."

"My current interest is all consuming, I'm afraid. But it is work related."

"How could that be of interest? I thought people read for enjoyment, relaxation, edification ..."

"Ah hah!" Aubrey said, "Edification. That is the key to success. That is what I have been aching to tell you, Mr. Flaherty. My work related study will benefit us both, I believe."

"I'm listening ..." Flaherty said.

"I have always been interested in exploring more deeply into the arcana of my profession. Adding more depth to it, so to speak. Not just the techniques of it, but the whole philosophical and psychological aspects as well. To add more gravitas to what I do. And you might be interested in this ... because I take my lead from you. To stop for a minute and examine what exactly are we doing? Are we doing it as best we can? Are we doing it with all the gusto of our beings? There is a need for creativity here. Some artistic gratification. Fulfillment if you will. I personally will never be satisfied with mere workmanlike production. A mundane approach bores me to death. I do have pride, as you well know."

Flaherty sat back in his chair and said "What the devil are we talking about here, John?"

"I've had this burning desire since I first had the good fortune of working for you. Frankly, what you want to do and what you want to accomplish for the Irish is so commendable. And your effort to remove any obstacle that might stand in the way of that goal ... well, I am so pleased to be an important spoke in the wheel of what you do. But ..." Aubrey again wiped his brow, neglecting the drool from his lip and leaned in closer to Flaherty, "But I have often asked myself is that enough? Shouldn't there be more? To add some element of art to the process?"

"Tell me what you are studying now Aubrey, before I fall off this chair."

"Why, torture of course," exclaimed the manager of the *Cherry Street Rotters*, "Philosophically, we have to ask ourselves is it enough just to exterminate our enemies? What pleasure is there in that, other than the finality of it all? Aren't some of them worthy of suffering just a little bit more than being the recipient of a quickly applied terminal death blow to the scalp? What pleasure is in it for us and what degree of pain is there for the recipient? There needs to be more genuine and prolonged suffering in special cases. Much more. I'm not talking about the Honeymelon Cabbages of this world although there are enough of them we could do without. I'm talking about those who are repeat offenders. The depraved, unrepentant sub-humans who consistently and unashamedly stand in the way of your dream. Our dream, Mr. Flaherty," Aubrey took a deep breath and asked, "May I trouble you for a spot of tea?"

"Why of course, John. How thoughtless of me not to have a pot ready for you," Flaherty said as he walked over to the potbelly stove and put a cast-iron kettle on the heat, "It should be ready for you in just a few minutes."

"First of all, I want to thank you for listening to me," Aubrey said, "I am very well aware of how busy you are."

"The pleasure is all mine. I am glad you have the confidence in my presence to be … ah, so vulnerable and … transparent. Only recently I mentioned to Peggy O'Rourke that she would enjoy a meaningful conversation with you. But as we're delving into this topic, I think I will hold off on that for the time being."

"She is a stunning woman, Mr. Flaherty. Statuesque. Stately. Aside from or even despite her physical virtues, I know she is of great help to you as a liaison with suppliers. But I have to confess that sometimes in the loneliness of my little room, I imagine her … I think of her … I picture her …"

"Yes?" Flaherty prompted.

"I just close my eyes and picture her without a stitch of clothing on. It would be hard for me to be in her presence, alone that is, because I would be so conflicted, at once overly conscious of my sinful nature, then irresistibly preoccupied with that persistent mental image of her that pops up quite frequently of late," Aubrey closed his eyes and blurted, "Wondering if there is a match to the color of her …"

"Tell me now," Flaherty interrupted, "What books you are presently studying?"

Aubrey opened his eyes and asked, "Are you familiar with the works of Donatien Alphonse Francois?"

"Can't say that I am," Flaherty said, walking over to pour the tea. He returned and placed two cups on a small table.

"Most people know him as the Marquis de Sade. I absolutely devoured his writings, poems, plays, essays, whatever I could get my hands on in all the little bookstores in the city. They take up a whole shelf in my little space."

"I do know of him but confess I have not read a word. I imagine you read the original French?"

"I do. Not as well as I would like but I get the drift of what the Marquis desired to communicate to our puritanical world."

Both men took a moment to enjoy their tea. "But it is the unintended work of another writer who has caught my attention of late," he said as he looked slyly at Flaherty.

"Unintended, you say?"

"He is an Irisher just like you. Visiting in France so many years ago and a keen observer of the way things were done in that lovely country. A man by the name of James Saint John, a traveler and diarist who certainly knew how to express his ideas in exquisite picaresque detail. His writing was unintended so to speak in that he was simply penning a letter to a friend in the late seventeen hundreds, unaware that his work would someday be good enough to be published and highly regarded by scholars of such subjects as he was observing."

"A scholar such as yourself, Mr. John Aubrey," Flaherty interjected.

"O, you do flatter me. I don't know if I would be considered a scholar. A serious student would suffice to say. What I found interesting about the work of Mr. Saint John, aside from the subject matter, of course, is that he apparently did not know his epistles would one day be encased in a book. Much like Paul the Apostle writing letters to the church in Ephesus, in Thessalonica, and others. The saint did not know at the time he was writing a goodly portion of the New Testament, for God's sake. Anyhow, this traveler wrote these simple but very explicit letters to a friend back home in the south of Ireland, describing the most delicious tortures dreamed up by creative minds. For instance, he writes about what he saw in Burgundy, outfitting a criminal with a pair of iron boots then pouring scalding oil into them between the flesh and the iron. Then he mosies on over to Strasbourg and Alsace where he witnesses a cold-water torture of the cruelest nature. Then to another part of France he was allowed to observe a criminal getting bound and seated in an iron chair that heats up quite considerably as the chair is strategically situated within the very center of an intense ring of fire. Saint John must have toured the entire country because he describes a man hogtied and suspended from this high barn ceiling with a strong string wrapped around his big toe. Threaded through a pulley system, the poor wretch is dropped, confined that way from different heights until at the very end they ratchet him up to the very top of the barn and let him go, but apparently his torturers carefully measured the physics of it all with dummies and weights so that with each drop of his body causes him to come ever so close to smashing his head on the floor. By the time it is over, the exquisite agony between his shoulder blades was enough to send him to the other side of pain. But my favorite – let me emphasize that I enjoy the creativity of these devices and techniques more than seeing a fellow human being suffer – but at Dijon, with mallets they drove wedges of oak between his knees and ... does anything strike you as odd about what I am telling you?"

"Well ... ah ..."

"I don't mean the details of the tortures ... but the fact that this man goes here, there and everywhere in a foreign land as if he's on holiday, that some agent arranged his dream trip where he would get to see all these incredible devices and applications ..."

"Oh, you mean ..."

"Yes! That's correct. Saint John must have been directly involved in the process of torture himself ... not just writing about them ... he is enacting them ... that is what I believe, but we'll never know, will we?" Aubrey said, taking another sip of tea, "By the way, this tea is delicious. Can you tell me does it have a name?"

" It's a blend of Chinese teas, as far as I know. Listen John, I believe that I need to head home in just a few minutes. I need to leave quite early tomorrow morning for the Capitol," Flaherty said.

"Oh, permit me just a few more moments as I don't want to leave you in suspense in terms of what the main point of my thesis is. Saint John reveals for those of us who follow that these were occasions of the most exquisite agony, great violence, horrible pain and ... don't you think that by his choice of words this Irishman was more than a spectator. It's not like the entire country of France decided to have a torture sideshow. I read between the lines and ...

in any event, these opportunities are available to us at minimal cost for supplies."

"That's very good to know, John. Keep up the good work. I'll let you know whenever I am especially troubled by one of my adversaries. Thank you. Most illuminating," Flaherty said as he donned his wide-brimmed hat and talma.

"One more thing before you go," Aubrey said as he stood up, "If you will be so kind. I have a confession to make. It involves Miss O'Rourke."

Flaherty sat down again. "What is it, John?"

"Remember years ago when you asked me to take care of some business overseas. A bit of justified retribution for the malicious treatment of the O'Rourke family ... how he summarily threw them out of their cottage in the middle of winter ..."

"Yes. Of course I remember. You confirmed to me at the time that you took care of their British landlord. I even recall reimbursing you for travel expenses. I decided that I could never tell Peggy about that, in as much I think she would have been satisfied to know that justice was done in her case, but she made that request of me as a bitter, angry, severely wounded adolescent ..."

"Oh, I think you made the right decision to withhold that information from her ... she might have been making that request of you rhetorically ... but there's another reason why I never told you about the details concerning that assignment. I regret I was not entirely forthcoming at the time. I withheld the total story from you all of these years because ... well, at times I meant to tell you ... but once I met Miss O'Rourke, I judged it prudent as the revelation of the landlord's demise might have given her an unfavorable opinion of me ..."

"Out with it, John. I need to be on my way."

"I did not have your permission at the time but I undertook the application of the very subject we're discussing at this exact moment."

"I gather you tortured the bastard?"

"Indeed, I did. In a very special way, as a matter of fact. Since he is or was fully British and I am only part British, part Irish and part Barbadian, I put aside my Britishness and paid him back with a centuries old British torture they inflicted upon their hapless Irish servants and slaves in ..."

"Barbados," Flaherty said, "And I know you're dying to tell me about the torture but as I am in a bit of a hurry. Can you give me the shortened version, please."

"Please don't think ill of me. I did take into consideration sound ethical principles which helped me determine that what I did and the manner in which I did it was quite apropos to make amends for the O'Rourke family. Knowing fully the history of British cruelty perpetrated upon the Irish for centuries, one of their cruelest deeds was the application of psychological warfare that has not changed in hundreds of years. Because it works so well. Let them be anathama! The same false promises the British landlord made to the unsuspecting O'Rourke family was a continuation of the lies they made to their Irish indentured servants in the 1600's. They shipped these vulnerable men, women, and children to Barbados, falsely promising them free housing, good wages and a plot of land at the end of their indentures. Sound familiar? The British are so consistently uncreative because the Irish are so without guile."

Flaherty settled back in his chair. Aubrey took another sip of his tea and continued, "Okay, quickly then, I tracked him down to a little village in the English countryside. A spot at the water's edge, known as Hayswater Cove. I hid in the woods for a day or so, waiting for my opportunity to pounce. It was just he and his wife, for no evil spawn issued forth from that union. Quite early one morning I trapped him as he entered the barn. I gagged him and subdued him with ropes. He was rather stout, obviously well-fed and proper dressed in the latest fashions, even that early in the morning. No casual dresser he. Though he was unable to speak, I asked him to shake his head this way or that if he happened to remember the O'Rourke family from Collooney Town, County Sligo, a mother with her two young daughters he sent off on a coffin ship and the husband and father he banished to a debtor's prison where he did die in the filth of that place. For his meager defense of these charges he shook his head no. In my opinion, granted it was a first impression meeting him in this aggressive manner, that he represented a typical example of Britain's outward manifestation of man's depravity. Concrete evidence that their pretentious show of civility and manners belies their utter lack of both. Their innate barbarism succeeded in turning some of the Irish into depraved human beings at times. But who made us that way? Was it not the British? Yes, at some point we have to take responsibility for our own actions. Hopefully it won't take centuries for that to happen. Look at you, Mr. Flaherty. You rescued many of the Irish from abject poverty, not the least of whom is the subject of this whole conversation, Peggy O'Rourke. You didn't indenture her. You gave her a golden opportunity. Look how well she's doing for herself and you. We are not animals."

Aubrey took a deep breath, as Flaherty poured more tea into both cups.

"Thank you. You are a godsend and by the way this is the best tea that ever entered my cruelly formed mouth. Forgive my diversions, Mr. Flaherty. You are truly a kind man … then I found the missus in the cottage, quite a chunky ball of flesh she was. Gave me more of a fight than her cowardly husband. Anyhow, being careful not to harm her physically, I gagged her and bound her to a kitchen chair so she would not alert the neighbors as I went about my business. Her eyes of fright are still clear to me to this day. While she sat in her chair, I made a small fire in their hearth. I grabbed a bucket from madam's pantry and drew water from their well. When the fire was blazing I turned and turned my branding iron until it glowed. I went back to the barn, pulled down mister's pantaloons and seared 'JA' with the hot iron into his bare bum. He squirmed considerably as the iron hissed upon his flesh. Considerably weakened by then, I untied him but kept his gag in place. I suspended him from a makeshift crossbar I affixed to one of the barn's supporting beams, making sure the tips of his big toes barely touched the ground. I flogged his bare back with well-placed blows, swinging the weapon left-to-right then right-to-left on its return. I did this repeatedly, without counting. I continued the whipping until he fainted. I laced the water in the bucket with salt and poured it over his naked back. When he regained consciousness the whipping continued. I made a rub with a mixture of vinegar and pepper and massaged it into his considerable wounds. The rest I will leave to your imagination. I did not linger to witness whether or not he drew his last breath. I left the limp body of a privileged

Englishman on the filthy barn floor. If he survived, I hoped the beating bought to the surface some faint memory of the O'Rourke family and encouraged him to make peace with his maker. I checked on his bride before departing. Although securely bound and gagged, she actually looked quite content, maybe discerning from my perspiring body that her husband got the worst of my visit. I left her sitting there with the cottage door wide open. Surely some neighbor came by later that day and freed her from her confinement."

"You're well suited for this work, John, I must admit."

"It is my pleasure Mr. Flaherty. I should let you be on your way. My delicious books await me and you need your sleep," John Aubrey said. He threw his cloak over his shoulders. He walked a few paces and said, "The Honeymelon Cabbage file will be complete within a day or two. At least the packaging part of it. If you don't mind, can I bother you for a small pouch of those tea leaves. I find favor with foods and drink that are blends. Like me. I'm not pure this or pure that. It's been a most delightful evening," he said, as Flaherty handed him the pouch, along with the stop order summons.

"What do you want me to do with this?" Aubrey asked.

"File it in the vegetable section, John."

"Thank you again for your time, Mr. Flaherty. Amongst other things that I take away from our conversation tonight, I am sensing the desire to learn more about tea leaves. Creating different blends of fine tea. Maybe some day, even coming up with my own brand. My own portion, so to speak."

"Regarding the Honeymelon Cabbage file, keep in mind that it's harder to dig when the ground is hard," Flaherty warned.

"True enough. Things take longer to rot when they are frozen, that's for sure. But eventually they still rot," Aubrey said as he exited the dome by the same trap door through which he had entered.

THE ELECTRICAL INSPECTOR

The doorbell rang. Frank ignored it. Go away, just go away, leave me alone was his singular wish. After a moment, it rang again. He opened the door but stood behind the screen, staring down at the man on the other side, all the while rocking back and forth, heel to toe, heel to toe, with his eyes opening and closing in rhythm with his body. Sweat poured down his brow, wetting his sideburns, coating his neck. Although it was close to two in the afternoon, Frank greeted this visitor while dressed in his robe and pajamas. "Wadda you want?" he demanded.

The man pointed to his photo i.d., attached to a ribbon looped around his neck. "My name is Hank Abbott, the town electrical inspector."

"Good for you. I'm glad you got a job but I didn't order any inspection. Get lost." Frank said. As he started to close the door, the inspector took a step closer and held up his clipboard, showing the address and the order for the scheduled inspection. Frank could see through the screen that it was his address, 305 Clarity Lane. At that, he slammed the door shut, but stayed in place, waiting for the inevitable. After a moment, the doorbell rang again.

Frank opened the door quickly, and screamed, "Get the hell out of here. I don't want to be bothered. Do you understand?"

Hank spoke softly, "Listen, Mr. Cohasco, I have a job to do. If it doesn't get done today, I'll have to keep coming back. There's no way around it. I have to finish the report."

"How else can I say this? Get off my property. Just leave me alone." Frank started to rock in place again. Hank noticed that the collar of the man's bathrobe was soaked in sweat. He stayed put on the bottom step. Frank persisted, "Do you want me to call the police?"

Hank moved up one step. "I don't think you want to do that."

"Give me one reason why not," Frank said.

Hank was now face-to-face with Frank, separated by only the thin screen. "Well," Hank said, again in a gentle, patient voice, "For one, we all kind of know each other. It's a small town, as you know Mr. Cohasco. The police barracks and the town hall share the same campus. An open hallway connects the buildings. We see each other every day. Actually, the police enforce our orders. But we don't have to get to that point. Why don't you just let me come in so I can explain what's involved with the inspection. It shouldn't take more than a half hour if all goes well."

Frank opened the screen door, allowing Hank to stand in the hallway, yet blocked him from going any further. Hank's senses were assaulted with a variety of foul odors. The smell of sour milk and moldy vegetables, mixed in with Frank's penetrating bad breath and body odor created a dense, inescapable atmosphere. The men were so uncomfortably close to each other that Hank could count the man's errant nose and earlobe hairs.

Frank continued in a belligerent tone, "You people just think you can come in here and do whatever the hell you want? What about my privacy? Aren't I entitled to that? I suppose you'll be like all the others and find an excuse to creep into the upstairs bathroom and examine my wife's underwear on the floor. Then, you'll open the medicine cabinet and have a good laugh, knowing what drugs we take. THAT'S NONE OF YOUR DAMN BUSINESS! UNDERSTAND?"

Hank simply responded, "I don't believe you have a wife, Mr. Cohasco."

Frank backed off a few steps into the kitchen area, stretching out both arms, grasping the counter tightly. "You see that. That's another problem. How did you know whether or not I have a wife? How do you know anything about me?" He moved closer to Hank again, and said in a whisper, "Do you know what happened to the last inspector?"

The men stared at each for a long moment. Hank broke the silence, "I'm not sure what you're getting at."

"Just watch yourself," Frank threatened, "Do what you have to do, then get out of here."

Armed with his clipboard, flashlight, pocket camera and ballpoint pen, Henry (Hank) Abbott, the town's electrical inspector, had a job to do. He started the inspection in the upstairs bathroom, uninterested in the contents of the hamper or the medicine cabinet. His only interests were the sockets, fixtures, and wires, making sure they all conformed to code. Next, Hank checked the two bedrooms on the second floor and the hall closet. It did not take long for Hank to estimate that this particular household tour would take two or three times longer than normal, as he had to sift through piles of garbage and stacks of magazines and books, just to see where the outlets were located.

Hank flipped a page on his clipboard and checked every room on the first floor: kitchen, living room, half bath, bedroom, Florida room, and the den where Frank settled into his La-Z-Boy, stupefied before the 72-inch flat screen TV, absorbing the 24-hour news cycle.

Next on Hank's checklist was the attached garage, by far the neatest space on the premises, with row after row of tarp-covered cartons and plastic containers. He peeked under a few of the covers to confirm what he had already suspected. Lastly, Hank examined every socket, wire and connection in the basement, taking several close-up pictures of the control box. He located every room or closet he needed to, except for one space that was currently inaccessible. He would report to Mr. Cohasco that everything so far was in compliance with the National Electrical Code.

Hank returned to the den where Frank had fallen asleep. He tapped him lightly on the shoulder. Frank pressed the OFF button on the remote and asked, "Are you done yet?"

"Just one more room."

"It's not that big of a house. Twenty six hundred square feet. No angles or curved hallways. Straight up and down. I think you've seen it all," Frank said with finality.

"Where can I find access to the attic crawl space?"

"Who said there was an attic?"

"I can see the vents from the street. I don't know if it's a finished room or just a big, empty space. Either way, I need to take a look."

Frank laughed. "That must be where the raccoons live. The whole family. I hear them every night, crawling around and scratching everything, probably pooping all over the place. No wonder the house smells so bad," Frank got up out of his chair and started walking toward the front door, thinking the inspector's visit was over, "they're nighttime critters, you know. They see in the dark. They don't need any light up there. Saves me on the electric bill."

"Are you going to tell me where the access is?" Hank said, "Let's just do this now, Mr. Cohasco. Is there a drop down ladder somewhere? Is there a concealed opening in one of the closets? Come on, you don't have to hide anything from me. Just tell me where I can gain access, so I can be on my way."

Frank took a moment to consider his choices. The inspector seemed to disappear, blending into the walls and the furniture. Frank detached himself from the reality of the situation, and by habit dismissed the notion that he was trapped. He was not one given to self-examination. He did not consider for a moment that he was doing anything wrong. He needed to rely on his resourcefulness. That was his strongest suit.

Frank stared for a long moment at the inspector's dangling i.d. badge: "Henry Abbott, Electrical Inspector. With an official number. And the town seal. The photo was taken some time ago, wasn't it?"

"Are you trying to stall me, Mr. Cohasco?"

"No. Nothing like that. I just thought we could work on a ..."

Hank interrupted, "Don't even go there."

"Go where?" Frank protested, trying his best to speak as softly and respectfully as the inspector, "Let me finish my thought. You didn't think for a minute that I would try to offer you ..."

"Okay. Sorry. Finish whatever you were going to say."

"Wanna be my friend?" Frank asked, with no hint of sarcasm or desperation.

The simple answer, Hank thought, is that the man's invitation, flowing from an obviously angry, hostile, and *unfriendly* persona, was a gambit, a ploy, a ruse. Hank could not think of enough words to pinpoint his reaction to the totally unexpected invitation. It would have been routine for a guilt-ridden, code-breaking individual to offer a bribe so that the inspector would just simply check off all the yes boxes. Hank experienced plenty of that kind of offer through the years. It would have been less common, and equally unexpected, for a homeowner to fess up that he paid no attention to the town rules governing the installation of electrical repairs or upgrades in an effort to save money in this hard economy by hiring an unlicensed electrician. He heard enough of those stories too. You know, so and so's brother-in-law can do it on the side for a fraction of the cost and I swear it's all safe and your house won't burn down. For a man, whose career was based on the foundation of checking boxes yes or no, Frank's request could not be answered based on logic or experience.

Although Hank did not see this question coming and was not prepared to answer it automatically, it gave him a certain perspective on the whole matter that might equally surprise Mr. Cohasco. On this particular inspection, Hank did not take his marching orders from his supervisor. This visit was not even scheduled. There were no complaints from neighbors, nor was there an application submitted for rewiring, upgrades on equipment, the addition of a dormer, or shed, a fire department report on a small electrical fire or any of the many possible reasons a premises would require an official inspection.

On one slow day in the office, with no inspections scheduled, Hank decided to catch up on some paperwork.

Some days you just had to do it. It was mindless, tedious work that at least served to put one's mind at ease. In the numbing process of thumbing through records in the office's trans file boxes, Frank stumbled upon a curious omission. 305 Clarity Lane simply did not exist according to the town's records. There were ample records for 303 and 307 on either side but no account number for the premises in between them nor was it listed as an abandoned property. Very odd. He rechecked the records, block by block. No record anywhere of an active account. Curious, perplexed, Hank drove by the 305 address on several different nights. The lights were always on, with the big screen TV visible to the street. Hank called a friend at the cable company and inquired about their customer at 305 Clarity Lane. No such account, the friend told him. It was a mystery he was determined to solve.

"Yes. I would very much like to be your friend," Hank said. This response gave Frank a sense of momentary peace. Through his unexpected response, Hank suddenly became a welcome visitor. There was something about the inspector's demeanor that put Frank at ease, that momentarily rescued him from drowning in the filth of his life, and, although he did not know it at the time, his house would soon be literally cleansed of the unhealthy atmosphere of debris, clutter, and bacteria-ridden garbage left behind wherever it had originally fallen.

For the moment, Frank did not sense any personal threat from Hank. His normal deep-seated cynicism diminished somewhat. He still knew he had to be careful, to not let his guard down completely, yet he was not at the point of total abandonment. He had special motives for soliciting the inspector's friendship and did not expect

Hank to be so quick to respond in a positive manner. What Hank said to him next surprised him even more.

"Mr. Cohasco ..."

"Call me Frank."

"Okay, Frank. Call me Hank," then, without hesitating and speaking in a perfectly natural manner, Hank asked the gruff, foul smelling homeowner ever so politely, "I wonder if you wouldn't mind if I moved into your house for a couple of weeks."

Frank cranked up the La-Z-Boy, popped out of the chair and stood face-to-face with Hank, looking down at him, as he was a good half-foot taller than the inspector. He started rocking again, heel-to-toe, heel-to-toe, eyes opening and closing, his nostrils flared as he struggled to find the words, but Hank again put him at ease with his simple explanation. "I'm in somewhat of a transition right now so I just need to stay somewhere until I get settled. Besides, I noticed that you could use a little help around the house. I'm very organized, and, with your permission, I could get this house in really good shape in no time."

Reassured, calm even, Frank sat down and did not feel the need to immediately reject or even protest Hank's request for temporary housing. "You can have either bedroom upstairs," Frank responded, "I sleep right here on my chair. You might have to move a few things out of the way to find the bed." A deeper sense of peace and contentment began to command his spirit from the tip of his toes to the top of his head. Normally a control freak, fortified by years of practice, he began to experience the pleasant, intimate sensation of allowing another human being to enter into his very private, secretive world. It never occurred to him, not even for one moment, that

Hank had any sinister motives, or was any different than the soft, gentle human being presented before him. Hank was unlike anyone he ever met. The man did not meet his aggression with aggression in return. Hank gave him a wide berth, granting him the space to settle down after his outbursts. He liked that. It was highly unusual.

On the other hand, little did Frank know that Hank had a master plan in mind. It was quite involved and complex but Hank thought better about springing it on his new friend for fear that the shock of the details would unnerve him and bring to a close the newfound friendship. He would let it unfold piece by piece, like honey dripping off a spoon.

Testing the uncharted waters, Frank said, "I could kick you out at any time, you know. It's my house."

"For sure. You have every right to do that. But I need some kind of commitment or I'll have to look elsewhere. How about a simple handshake that we have a deal." The two men shared a firm handshake, "We should celebrate our new friendship," Hank said.

"I think I have a bottle of gin lying around somewhere," Frank suggested, "But I don't think you're the kind of guy who'd drink straight out of the bottle. I don't know if I have any clean glasses."

"Let me go to the store and get a few bottles of beer," Hank said, already moving toward the door.

Defaulting to his suspicious frame of mind, not wanting Hank to leave the premises with his clipboard and report, Frank rose out of his chair, beating Hank to the door, "How about if I go with you?"

"No need to. Stay in your pjs" Hank insisted, leaving his clipboard and car keys on the side table near Frank's chair, anticipating that Frank was nervous about what would happen once he headed back to the office, "I'll just walk around the corner to the deli. I'll be right back."

The instant Hank left the house, Frank glanced at the report. He was relieved that nothing unusual stood out. He was especially interested in what the inspector had to say about the garage, but, to his surprise, it was just another checked box that everything was in order. Not fully satisfied, however, he stepped into the garage and saw that everything remained undisturbed. It was the cleanest space on the premises, several rows of tarp-covered boxes, secured with bungee cords. Of course, he had no way of knowing if Hank peeked under the tarps, but gave his new friend credit for being an incurious professional just going about his business of checking outlets, fixtures, cords and wires, desiring to know little else. His new friend. Just doing his job.

Hank returned with beer and potato chips. The new buddies clinked bottles and toasted their new friendship. Frank experienced a sense of well-being. Not that he entertained any thought of doing such a thing any time soon; he was delighted he did not have to clean up the house on his own. The unsightly mess he lived in did not in the least bit embarrass him. After all, it is his house and his world, such as they are, chaotic, unclean, smelly, a joyous pigsty of a home.

If any bugs crawled over Hank's face at night, it was not his fault. Hank invited himself into his world, not the other way around. Frank felt good about himself, generous even, opening up his home to someone who, only three hours earlier, was a total stranger to him. How many people would agree to such an arrangement, he wondered.

Frank asked his friend if he needed to collect any personal belongings before he moved in. Without going into too much detail, Hank told him that everything he needed was already in the trunk of his car. Hank expressed his gratitude and even offered to pay rent but Frank refused. He could hardly stand himself for being so generous all of a sudden. The men drank the beer slowly and chatted about the news, sports and the weather.

Henry Abbott, Master Electrician. That was his dream growing up, to hear those words spoken about him, a man who had the skills and training to light up the world. Before Hank appreciated the beauty and majesty of electricity, he learned about its power when he was just a toddler. Left alone by his mother for just a moment, and all it takes is a moment for a child to get into trouble, little Henry crawled along the floor and found a two-pronged electrical plug under the lamp table. It was something his father must have left behind while doing home repairs. Flowing out of the end of the hard rubber plug was a two-inch spray of frayed wires, shaved back from its rubber coating. Crawling closer to the corner nearest the table, the curious little boy sat up, held the new toy in his hand and spotted a wall socket with two slits that appeared to be just as wide a space as the two-pronged device he held in his hand. He thought it would be just a grand idea to make a match and jam it into the opening. And jam it he did. The power of the unimpeded electrical shock threw him back three feet and stung his fingers with a sensation more memorable than ten angry bees. His tiny hand was black, blue and red for weeks.

From that highly memorable moment forward, Hank had maintained the highest respect for electricity. Next up for him on his path to Master Electrician was the Christmas gift of an American Flyer train set, complete with tracks, a transformer with so many different dials and an engine car that turned pellets into real smoke as it choo-chooed around the track, hauling eight cars and a caboose, hours upon hours of excitement generated by electricity.

Unlike most people, who, at some point, take electricity for granted, Hank possessed an undying appreciation for motion and sound sensor lights. Just clap and the lamp goes on. Hank never lost the fascination for the power and beauty of what humankind had been able to harness, mostly for the good of others.

As Frank droned on about the local news, Hank's mind wandered into a recent fascination of his, the phenomenon of bioluminescence. From his childhood, he knew that fireflies, squid and some species of mushrooms glowed in the dark. He studied how these creatures produced light and believed, along with others, that it could offer a path to solving the economic and ecological issues presented by electrical lighting. The subject of bioluminescence as a chemical reaction encouraged by genes, fascinated him. Some enterprising start-up companies were experimenting with common bacteria, which grow to create a material that produces a stable light. As Frank reported on all the local news, Hank looked at the unhealthy mess occupying every inch of the house and fantasized that there was enough bacteria in just one of these rooms to light up a city.

When Frank paused from echoing what was being broadcast on TV, Hank questioned his new buddy about his background, what it was like growing up in Brooklyn, New York, which he mentioned earlier in their conversation. "I had a terrible childhood," Frank said, "I hated my parents. I hated the neighborhood. I hated the schools they made me go to." There was a long moment of awkward silence, giving Hank the understanding that it was better not to ask what he did for a living.

Then the doorbell rang. Having it ring twice in one day was almost too much for Frank as he shot out of his chair, spilling the chips on the floor, now keeping company with the rest of the bacteria and debris. He rushed to the door, yelling, "Who the hell is it?" as he yanked the it open.

As was his habit, Frank stood safely behind the screen door, and again rocked back and forth, his eyes unconsciously opening and closing as he spoke, this time in a less aggressive manner than when he first greeted Hank earlier in the day. "Who are you?" he asked of the beautiful, blond-haired woman standing on the other side.

"I'm Hannah from Hamburg," she answered, laughing.

"Yeah, and I'm Frank from Flatbush."

By this time, Hank stood right next to Frank, and he spoke on the woman's behalf, "Hannah's my wife. You can let her in. She's harmless."

Reluctantly, Frank opened the screen door and Hannah walked in, nearly brushing up against Frank as she moved toward her husband. Not fully grasping what would come next, Frank was not displeased with the vibrancy and freshness Hannah displayed in her manner and in the sweet, flowery clean aroma of her hair that came within inches of his nose. Her eyes opened widely as she surveyed the clutter and filth, "I see the three of us have a lot of work ahead of us."

"The three of us?" Frank asked as he looked at Hank.

"This is a great day, Frank. First, you find a new male friend and in the same day you gain a new female friend."

"Will she ..." Frank started to say.

"She'll stay in the same room with me," Hank said, anticipating Frank's concerns, which were many.

"But ..." Frank wanted to protest, part of him not caring one bit about Hank sleeping in a bug-infested room, but another part of him, for a long time untouched and mostly unexplored, caring that such a fresh-smelling, attractive female would think less of him for his lack of attention to cleanliness.

"Look at it this way," Hank explained, "I don't want to stereotype, but Hannah is first generation, pure-stock German. That means she is well organized, knows how to clean to absolute white-glove perfection, and for an added bonus, makes a worldclass Sauerbraten."

"I guess it'll be all right as long as she can cook and clean for us," Frank said dully.

"Oh no I won't!" Hannah said cheerfully, "Hank and I will show *you* how to do it. It'll be the three of us. Together as a team."

"Except the Sauerbraten," Hank added quickly, looking admiringly at his wife.

Hannah walked into the kitchen, followed by the two men. "We have to get this stove cleaned, then clear the sink of all the dirty dishes," looking straight into Frank's twitching eyes, "I wash, you wipe, okay."

"Okay. I guess so," Frank answered, learning so much in such a short period of time.

The two men retreated into the den while Hannah went upstairs to see what challenges loomed ahead of her in the two bedrooms. About forty-five minutes later she came downstairs, beads of perspiration matting her hair, both arms loaded down with dirty sheets and pillowcases.

She told the men she was headed to the Laundromat and when she got back she would need their help to clear the two rooms of anything that looked like it was still alive or could be a cozy habitat for vermin. Frank promised to find the vacuum that was somewhere in the basement. Hannah ran down a list of supplies she planned to purchase, including white vinegar, disinfectant, contractor bags and so on, plus an assortment of food items that immediately stirred Frank's appetite, otherwise accustomed to fast food and frozen dinners.

Feeling mildly guilty that Hannah was tackling so much work, he said, "Don't bother with the second room. Just work on your own. I sleep right here," pointing to his big chair, "Been doing it for years."

"Oh no, you must not do that any longer, Mr. Cohasco. It's a beautiful fall day. I opened the windows so you can get a delicious cross breeze. The room faces south so your day will be filled with healthy sunshine. You'll wake up refreshed each morning, hearing the birds sing. More importantly, sleeping on a real bed is better for your posture. You're a tall man but I bet that once you get out of that chair, you'll be a full two inches taller. You won't be bent over from sleeping in a chair every night."

Frank never liked to be told what to do but it was impossible to argue with anything Hannah said. The main thrust of what she and her husband expressed was all to his benefit. How could he argue with them? They had such a trustworthy manner, he found it hard to criticize them. He did not feel the need to establish his dominance, even in light of the fact he was not in charge of what was taking place around him. Things were happening so fast, mostly without his input, so he felt compelled to say something.

He climbed out of his chair, stretched to his full height in front of Hannah, taking pleasure in her acknowledging that he was a tall man. "Will you ..." Frank said, "If you don't mind ... will you ... call me Frank?"

"I'll call you Frank," Hannah said, laughing, "In fact, I'll call you Frank from Flatbush. I like the sound of that."

The weariness from a hard life and the creases in Frank's peeling bark face disappeared as he smiled, "That's fine, as long as I can call you Hannah from Hamburg." The three of them laughed. The mood in the formerly grim house changed from shades of dark gray into light pastels. Hank turned off the screen on the big TV and tuned into a music station that added to the home's new upbeat atmosphere. In a matter of hours, the spirit within 305 Clarity Lane evolved from a house of horrors to a house filled with light, music and laughter. The open windows, the pleasant chatter, and aromas from the stove in the cleaned-up kitchen filled the downstairs level with pleasant surprises for all the senses.

That night Frank, fully horizontal for the first time in years, surrounded by the smell of fresh sheets, found himself confessing that it was good to have a woman around the house. Yet he still had trouble sleeping, conflicted with the swiftness of his newfound friendships coupled with the real possibility Hannah and Hank were on to his secret life. Things were too pat. The couple was too perfect, like cutouts from *Better Homes and Gardens*. He rationalized that if they had revealed to the authorities what they already knew, he would have been in handcuffs hours ago. Still restless, he got out of bed, took a few steps into the hallway, and then stood still, as if to avoid disturbing a dangerous animal in the forest.

Illuminated by subdued night-lights, Hannah stood in the portal of the bathroom, with one arm raised, her hand gripping the doorjamb, the other hand resting on her hip, her legs casually crossed. As a living tableau of a Klimt painting, the fullness of Hannah's voluptuous body showed itself to Frank, alluringly veiled by the sheerest of nightgowns. Frank avoided eye contact for fear he would miss one detail of her stunning figure, the full breasts, the prominent nipples, the soft pelvis driving down to the triangular nest of hair. It might have lasted but a mere minute before Hannah headed back to her bedroom, but Frank knew then that this heavenly vision would last a lifetime for him. He leaned against the wall as involuntary secretions ran down his thigh. Unrepentant, willing to betray his new male friend, Frank imagined, in frenzied, irrational thought, that he would do away with Hank just to have Hannah for his very own.

Frank compared himself to Hank, a short, stout, bald man, with hairy legs, and wanted Hannah to know that he was physically fit, albeit from many nights digging tunnels and climbing telephone poles, acquiring numerous splinters and creosote stains in his strong hands, which now wanted to hold her tight. Before he fell asleep, he mentally reviewed the highlights of his nights of resourcefulness when wires were spliced and telephone poles were climbed, the many splinters taken out with tweezers and a magnifier; the pounding of his chest, the loss of breath when he thought every police siren he heard signaled a chase after him. Frank's mind could not trace back to the exact moment he turned to a life of thievery, and then even more poignantly, to the pivotal point where he gave no thought whatsoever to the notion that he was doing anything wrong.

Frank's fantasy about Hannah dominated his thoughts. The final item he recalled before succumbing to dreamland, was vowing to appear for the breakfast Hannah from Hamburg would surely make, fully showered, shaved and dressed in garments other than his soiled pajamas.

When Frank awoke in the morning, he did clean up but cast aside any notion of a romance with Hannah from Hamburg. Instead, his heart and mind were heavy with the acknowledgement of missed opportunities with women and with life.

A full week went by, devoid of any further hallway glimpses of Hannah's gorgeous body. The time was filled with rigorous cleanup work that Frank engaged in as an equal partner. Each day started with a full European breakfast, complete with a variety of sausage, bacon, chocolate croissants, eggs, deli meats, cheeses, and more, followed by a light lunch, and a memorable German feast for dinner. Hannah joked that the Germans never caught on to lite cuisine, as that would be the ultimate oxymoron.

Hannah succeeded in teaching Frank how to make simple, healthy meals. The long-range plan was for him to be self-sufficient after their departure. In the near term, he would be the head chef for their final days together. She even helped him create a menu so he could put a shopping list together and know what to buy at the market. They all had a good laugh when Frank took the Sunday paper and clipped coupons. The work they did was made less onerous with breaks that Hank called 'chips and beer' renewals.

Along the way, Frank learned the reasons why Hannah truly loved Hank. They had a love that went beyond lust and was so deep-rooted and genuine that

Frank saw them truly as one person, inseparable, devoted entirely to one another.

Late that evening, on the seventh day of their acquaintance, resting in the living room, with their feet up, seemingly without a care in the world, Frank thought about asking them to stay longer. Before he could speak, Hank put down the book he was reading and said, without the slightest trace of accusation or recrimination, "Frank, Hannah and I were talking and agreed that we can't leave until we help you with the last two rooms."

"There's just the garage," Frank said defensively, "And everything in there is already neatly stacked."

Hannah spoke, "Frank, don't you want to make your life easier and eventually be able to park your car in there?"

"I can leave it on the street," Frank said.

Hannah then left the room so the two men could work out the final details of their arrangement. She also did not want Frank to feel embarrassed or emasculated because of her presence. She knew that Hank would handle the situation in the most delicate manner.

"Listen, Frank," Hank said, "Here's the plan for the garage. I'm going to rent a cargo truck. We'll create a map that logistically will allow us to maximize our time on the road. Then, we'll load up all the packages in such a way that we start with the house the furthest away and work our way back home."

Frank, noticeably shocked, doubly by Hank's matter-of-fact presentation and by the realization that he and Hannah knew all along he was a thief. He tried to offer an explanation but Hank continued, "It's important that we do this under the cover of night and do it all in one run. This way, all the surprised homeowners will find a package on their front steps that they all but gave up for lost. If the delivery spills over to another day, we run the risk of the police and the news media going on red alert. We want to do this as discreetly as possible. What do you say, Frank? Can I have your okay on this plan?"

"What about this big TV and other things I've already been using," Frank asked.

"Why don't you wait on that, Frank? Get yourself a legitimate job, and then, to ease your conscience, maybe you can send anonymous postal money orders to these people. There are several ways you can reimburse the people you stole from. But emptying the garage will give you a good head start," Hank stopped talking for a moment and made sure he made direct eye contact for the next thing he had to say, "A head start on paying back and a head start on getting a real life for yourself."

Frank was beginning to feel a sense of freedom, rather than the misery of being caught rehanded. "You said two rooms."

"Yes," Hank responded in a way that revealed he knew everything about Frank's private life, "I found my way up to the crawlspace in the attic. That's quite a nest of wires and cables you got up there. You have to keep a low profile for the immediate future, but you would make one hell of an electrician. I can't say that I admire your work because that would be dishonest on many levels."

"What can we do about that?" Frank said.

"First thing we do is cut every wire and cable so you stop running up your neighbors' electric bills. The way you did it, spreading the connections around to several different premises, probably prevented any alarm bells going off. Also, I have a good buddy at the cable company.

You can pay them back over a period of time. Be a good neighbor. Offer to mow lawns, run errands for old ladies, that kind of thing. Listen, we have all this week to think things through and work things out. We can do it. You can do it."

"What do I do for electricity after the wires are cut?"

"I got that on my list," Hank said reassuringly, "I'll get you hooked up legally and you'll have an account and get a monthly bill. Anything else we should know about?"

Frank did not answer. He cupped his head in his hands, weeping in compulsive fits and starts.

In the days that followed, Frank slipped into a deep depression. With Hannah and Hank holding up mirrors to what a normal, decent life looks like, it brought him to a dark place, not fully understanding why he dived so deep into dangerous crimes. It might have been better had he been caught somewhere along the way, but he got so good at it, it became a thrill each time he tried something more daring. He continually challenged himself to become more and more deceptive, to the point that this is who and what he became. Thievery and deception defined him. Because of Hannah and Hank's friendship, he discovered that he had a conscience after all, it being enough of a portion that it lead him into a bout of self- loathing. Hank and Hannah were successful in keeping him out of prison, but now he became frightened, not knowing what step to take next.

When Hank and Hannah noticed that Frank kept sinking deeper into despair, Hank took Frank aside: "I'm no psychologist, Frank, but I think you'd better see someone to talk about things. Once we clear out all this stuff, you might be tempted to start up bad habits all over again. You'd be better off if you get to the root of your issues."

Hank and Hannah kept busy planning the cargo run to return the stolen goods and working out the other details that would leave Frank with some semblance of a life. By the middle of the week, Frank decided that, until he could figure out what traumatic event in his previous life experience turned him into a thief, he would be proactive in living each day in a positive way. He wanted to show his deep appreciation to his best and only friends before they parted ways.

On their last night together, Frank made dinner and insisted that he clean up afterwards by himself, to show them that he reached some level of self-sufficiency. Mr. and Mrs. Abbott were to do nothing but sit back and enjoy. Frank made meatballs and marinara sauce from scratch. He cooked the spaghetti exactly the way it was specified on the box. He bought a nice red wine to go with the meal. Although Hank and Hannah complimented him on the meal, Frank acknowledged that it was not even close to what Hannah fed them for two weeks.

"Don't be ridiculous," Hannah said encouragingly, "I've been cooking all my life. I learned from my mother who learned from her mother. You made an excellent meal, Mr. Frank from Flatbush. When we leave tomorrow, we'll be happy knowing that you're not going to be sitting in front of the TV eating frozen dinners every night."

"I'm not making any long-range plans. One day at time," Frank said, "But I know tomorrow I'll be going to the mall to see if any stores need a stock boy or clerk or if the restaurants need someone to flip burgers. I'll take two jobs if I have to." Frank started to tear up when he looked directly at his friends and spoke in an awkward but sincere way, "Thanks to both of you, I can do these things. I can wake up in the morning and not want to STEAL!"

Then morning came. Hank and Hannah told Frank they needed to skip breakfast and be on their way. Frank took Hank aside and told him he had to share some personal stuff. He stumbled through a few awkward sentences and admitted to Hank that he felt disgusted with himself that on the one night he encountered Hannah in the hallway that he lusted after her. Hank forgave him immediately and patted him on the shoulder. Then Frank said the following, which was even more difficult to admit, "I hate to intrude but I called the Town Hall yesterday and inquired about an inspector named Henry Abbott or Hank Abbott. They told me that they don't have anyone employed by that name." Frank nervously started rocking on his heels again, and asked, "Who are you?"

Hank, in his gentle, non-threatening way answered him, "Frank, the only way I can answer that is by asking, 'Who are you?' The three of us worked really well these last two weeks and everything you stole has been or will be returned except for the most important item."

"Which is?"

"Remember our earlier conversation when you made reference to the last inspector?" Hank said.

Frank knew where this was headed. "I can't return that item," he said.

"This might be your thorn in the side, Mr. Cohasco. You can never return a man's stolen identity."

"Did you know him?" Frank asked.

"Yes. I knew Conrad Harry Scofield very well, Mr. CO HA SCO. We were close. But things didn't turn out well for him or his wife. Their lives were ruined. They lost everything, their good name, even their will to live."

With that being said, Hank joined Hannah who was already in the passenger seat. Frank rested his hands on the car door. Hank turned on the ignition and rolled up the windows, freeing Frank's grip. As the car started moving slowly down the street, Frank ran after them, calling out, "YOU MADE ME A NEW MAN. BUT WHO AM I? WHO AM I?"

LIVE MUSIC TODAY

We met in the pysch ward about three years ago. That's when she told me that she had information the police would find helpful, significant details about a major crime committed in the vineyard where she worked. I was admitted to the hospital because I recently experienced a few psychotic episodes. I need to point out that I was not a regular. She was a regular. All the psychiatrists knew her. All the nurses knew her. All the occupational therapists, psychologists, and medical students knew her. She was a difficult patient. One of the nurses once made an offhanded remark to that effect, mumbling as she left her room. I was the only other patient O.G. talked to, aside from herself. Not that O.G. trusted me. I never asked her too many questions or offered any unsolicited advice. I just listened. O.G. respected that. She gave her psychiatrist a hard time and got switched around from one doctor to another because she was so difficult. Her main thing was that she would only reveal personal information if it was reciprocal. She would cooperate with them as long as it worked both ways. If the doctor was willing to open up and share all sorts of intimate information, she would do the same. Of course, that never happened.

Sometimes, she would tell me, a few of the male psychiatrists told her personal stuff. She surmised that they were just throwing the bull. She guessed that they made up some juicy details about themselves because they wanted to appear more interesting than they really were so she would be drawn to them and agree to have sex. Other female patients on the floor told me they did have sex with some of the doctors, despite the doctors knowing full well how unethical it was and that they risked forfeiting their medical licenses, so I figured they were full of crap, even though one of them produced a used condom as evidence. She told me to put it in a zip lock bag and pass it along to her sister who visited on Saturdays. She would then ask her sister to arrange for a DNA test once she was able to steal a comb from the same doctor. It was a wild story and I did not believe her. How could you believe anyone who was delusional most of the time? Yet I believed O.G.'s story about the big crime committed in the winery.

Anyhow, unlike the supposed predatory male doctors, I never had the desire to have sex with O.G. I thought she was dangerous. I know it sounds shallow, but I could tell that she was probably physically attractive at one time, equipped with a nice figure and soft, buttery skin. But the psychotropic drugs took their toll. The last time we were together, her once smooth skin was all pocked and her figure resembled a refrigerator box. By the way, O. and G. are not her real initials. Obviously, I would never reveal her name, but I felt the need to fake her initials as well. She is a real person, however. Very real. And very dangerous. My initials are W.T. F., no relation to any psychiatric patient you may know, dead or alive. Same goes for O.G.

Right now, I'm sitting in a pizza parlor on the Main Road, just a few booths away from her. I have not seen her in a few years but I'm reluctant to make eye contact. I don't know if she would even recognize me. I lost a lot of weight recently and I have a lot less hair. She looks quite different now. I can't quite put my finger on it, as I am making every attempt to avert her occasional glances. If she does spot me, she might be reminded of all the unpleasantness she was forced to go through at Easthaven Hospital. Also, I will represent to her the embodiment of her disease, a co-conspirator in the war against mental illness. She, like the rest of our particular population, simply wants to blend in, to be like everyone else crossing the street, waiting in line at the grocery store, doing everyday things, normal things, sane things in an ordinary, boring, day to day fashion. I could blend in. In fact, I could just disappear in a crowd. That would never be her case, however. She is too bright a star, as brilliant as she is sick. In an effort to save her mind, the psychotropic drugs prescribed for her took a heavy toll on her body. They did not so much as control her, or even dim her mind, but they did agitate her by revealing a disturbing knowledge of self. I was dying to talk to her but I kept my distance, obscuring my face with a napkin, a slice of pizza, and other people's heads that blocked our direct line of vision. She is sitting there in the booth, alone, constantly looking over her shoulder as if expecting someone to join her for a slice.

My purpose in telling this story is to convey the tale O.G. told me about the crime she witnessed. I did not know whether or not to believe her story at first. After all, she is nuts. I do not use that term in a cavalier, politically incorrect, insensitive or even disrespectful way. That's the exact term Dr. A, Chief of Psychiatry at Easthaven, chose to use one Friday morning at rounds, with twenty people sitting around the big table witnesses to that unnerving indiscretion. A nurse friend told me that. I owe her one. That's priceless. Who would of thunk it? The head shrink at a big hospital. The people around the table did not even blink when they heard that term even though it spilled out in such a professional setting. Even I know that term would never be found in the PDM. Dr. A probably used it before, about other difficult patients.

On that particular morning, when the nurses were giving detailed summaries of what took place in the ward the night before, they shared details, in perfunctory clinical voices, about Patient A being administered so many mgs of Thorazine or Risperdal, how Patient B responded to his electric shock treatment, Patient C refusing to shower all week, etc. and all sorts of medical jargon employed to describe each person's behavior and the circumstances surrounding that behavior. But when the conversation got around to O.G., and what she did or did not do, Dr. A. succumbed to street vernacular and summarized the whole instance by saying she was nuts. I never did find out what O.G.'s behavior was that prompted the head of psychiatry at a prominent psychiatric institution to use such an inappropriate layman's term. My nurse friend was discreet and did not reveal any confidential details. I can only imagine it was something big, if not dangerous.

I listened to O.G.'s story over the course of several weeks, delivered in chapters during the course of our involuntary stay at Easthaven. We had plenty of time on certain days, after meetings with our shrinks, O.T. sessions, art classes, chess games, and so on. We had free time to do whatever we wanted, but always in the common room. We were never allowed to be together in each other's room. I could choose to go to my room during free time and be alone and O.G. could do the same as long as it was her room she went to. But we sat close together in the common room when she decided to tell me her story. She did not bother to whisper because the other patients within hearing proximity did not care to hear what she had to say. They, like Dr. A, thought she was the lower case 'n' word most of the time. Also, they had their own weird fantasies and stories to tell or were satisfied to just sit and stare at ceiling tiles. O.G.'s reputation as a nut was no secret in the unit. Most of the other patients could not be bothered with her, mainly because they were bothered by her. They thought she was an intellectual phony, had airs about her, affected a superior attitude because she boasted about earning several advanced academic degrees. That is probably another reason she confided in me. I did not think she was a phony. I was not exactly her friend but at least I did not scramble to the other side of the common room or dining hall every time she showed up. Yet, she provided such specific details that made me pay close attention. After awhile, I did believe her. I knew some of the characters in her story and most of what she told me was easy to check out.

I am now going to let her tell her story as she told it to me whenever she was lucid. Some parts, the times she slipped into her psychosis will be filled in by what my nurse friend revealed to me or what rode the rails on the rumor mill train. Those parts of her story will erupt with a sudden change of voice in the narrative, as she descends into darkness, falling into the abyss she heroically tried to climb out of, time after time. Those paragraphs uncovering her dark periods will not be parenthetical. By necessity, they will be woven into the tapestry of her tale about the circumstances leading up to the crime and the crime itself. After all, that's who she is, sane one moment, then the biggest nut in the nuthouse the next. Those episodic details or asides will not necessarily be about the story she was so anxious to reveal to me. Those instances and terrors will be forever unknown to me, perhaps even to her self, of the hideous demons that crawled through her psyche bent on chaos and destruction, given birth in the past, the present and within the fear of any kind of future. They might come across as incoherent and out of place at times but, below the surface, they will always be about her heroic struggle with the reality of mental illness, often seeming like a losing battle, a boxing match with elusive shadows. My peculiar condition I plan to keep to myself. This is not about me. I believe O.G wants me to tell her story this way. She does not want anyone to get away with murder.

<u>O.G.'s Story</u>

My first day in my new position as Vineyard Manager was spent in a small cottage provided for me on the grounds of the 84-acre B&J Winery. It sat at the southernmost edge of the property, just sixty some odd feet from the edge of the cove, with a clear view of the water that flowed in, then emptied out to the bay. It was the beginning of March and a Nor'easter blew sheets of sleet and rain against the windows for hours before the heavy snow came. The only signs of life were three ducks frenetically diving in the water, in search of food. They seemed to enjoy the wild weather, which also suited me. It matched my temperament.

I believe I found a home as well as a place of employment. A vineyard run well is its own reward. It beats with a lively pulse and a healthy heart. My background included several summers spent interning at a few of Napa Valley's most prestigious commercial vineyards. I graduated with a degree from UC Davis, home of America's foremost program in viticulture and oenology. Following that, I obtained an advanced degree at the University of Bordeaux, then I took back-to-back intensive tours at wineries LaFleur Pomerol and Chateau Haut-Brion in France.

After I completed these tours, word about my availability got around very quickly back in the States. There was a lot of interest in my services at the wineries on the east coast. And, why not? It was a bit arrogant on my part but I decided that I did not have to trouble myself putting together a resume. A few Tweets retweeted, an email here and there, and a text message or two landed several serious offers. I accepted the offer at B&J because the two wealthy brothers who owned the vineyards had already poured the foundation for my dream of transforming a large chunk of arable real estate into a world class wine producing region. Between them, they knew the business side and the winemaking side of the enterprise, each brother boasting a serious Napa Valley pedigree. I accepted their offer above the many others that came my way, knowing that they were just as cocksure as I was about the lasting impact that could still be made on the national, even international world of fine wines. The brothers had a long way to go before they could achieve some serious bragging rights but their brazen vainglory impressed me. They saw me as a shortcut to that illustrious goal. I took the long view and planned to show them how to get to where they wanted to go.

In effect, the overwhelming majority of the wineries in this region were presently little more than a joke on the national level, with pretty accurate references to the region's wines, for example, as Deer Piss Chardonnay, Skunk Juice, Battery Acid Rose and my favorite, Bat Blood Reserve. By the way, did anyone ever make note of the fact you never find a dead bat on the ground on any given morning. We see dead birds, dead rodents and dead deer but never dead bats. Does a special cleanup crew in golf carts scour the vineyards just before dawn to collect their carcasses? We know the bats are there. We hear them at night. Do the owls eat them entirely, fur, feet and bones all gone before sunrise? Owls eat small birds and rodents too. We are witness to their remains on the ground. Just some idle thoughts about what goes into the production of a less than stellar beverage.

The more cynical folk out this way say they know people who follow winery employees into the local IGA to watch them buy packaged grapes. I doubt that is true. Nonetheless, the brothers Barth and James know, and I know, and they know I know, it is going to take more than arrogance and lackadaisical daydreaming to make consistently good, much less great wines in this region. It will take consistent arrant behavior on all our parts, the three of us working pertinaciously together to show it can be done, to diminish, defeat even, the perception that this wine region should not even exist. Whenever one of the local vintners actually manages to produce a somewhat palatable wine, it is invariably outrageously overpriced. All one has to do is visit a local retail store to find a California wine of comparable quality selling at one third the price.

Most of the region's wineries make their money or at least break even by succumbing to the tourist and wedding destination crowds that have built up over the last several years. Signs such as LIVE MUSIC TODAY, BUSES AND

LIMOS WELCOME, and WEDDING OPEN HOUSE pollute the landscape. Hiring way past their prime hippie folk singers ceaselessly droning somewhat familiar tunes of yesteryear will simply not cut it. Consume enough wine, look at the pretty scenery and life is good.

One winery was daring enough to offer a BORDEAUX MASTER CLASS. Can you imagine? Just who is the master at the blackboard I ask. Give me a break. Forgive me; I admit I am a wine snob. The visitors, for the most part, gulp instead of sip, get drunk fast, and convince themselves the next morning they had a meaningful visit to the vineyards. They might have even taken a tour. And, they brought home a case or two, committing to an unfortunate one-year's subscription of a monthly delivery of six whites and six reds of unknown quality. Ultimately, they always fail to taste as good as when the music played and the elm leaves swayed in the lovely sea breeze.

Barth and James were aware of this universal negative perception about the region's output held by their west coast peers. There was little hope they could ever stand shoulder to shoulder with the California vintners, under the system that was then in place, but they wanted to give it a try. Something significant had to take place, a radical plan had to be put in motion to make something positive happen. It is not saying much but B&J was easily the class of the region – no skunk juice appellation here but they did manage to produce their share of mediocre wines.

What intrigued the brothers about my resume was my specialty, clonal regeneration, in particular French grapes. We could produce genetic variants of grape varieties that have been developed and propagated to emphasize particular characteristics such as aroma, flavor, or yield. I knew what to do and how to do it. It would take a lot of money, which they had, and a lot of time which was generally okay with Barth but not so much with his business-oriented brother James. Therein lies part of the reason why things did not go as planned, why they sabotaged themselves in the grandiose effort to enter under the golden arches onward through the gateway to the world of fine wines.

At last I am in control! I know exactly what is going on at every moment. They could pour that poisonous gas through the floor vents in the cottage and I will not be fooled. I know for certain that it is the same gas they poured through the ceiling vents at Easthaven. I see the vapors. I do not have to smell them. Clever, aren't they? I had to empty everything out of the refrigerator too. Did they think I would be fooled by a sealed bottle of water? Liquid poison! They were especially cruel this time. After I cleared every single thing out of that refrigerator, the last remaining item on the bottom shelf that I had to get on my hands and knees to fetch, was a bottle of 7UP, lying on its side. Clever! But I did not fall for it. Not this time.

Maybe it was my parents who made me sick. They are long dead, thank God. When I was in high school, I studied so hard I rose to the top of the class. Whenever I came home with my report card extolling exceptional grades, the only person in the household who appreciated that honor was me. Many of my friends wrote such genuinely warm messages and honorific reminiscences under their photos, even more on the blank pages in the back of the yearbook. Every now and then, I had to check my parents' entry in the yearbook to make sure it was actually their handwriting. It was and is. They signed it. It was a generic to and from message, ending coldly with Mother and Father. Even the classmate who liked me the least, the one I beat out by a few percentage points for valedictorian honors, signed her message 'warmly'. The other girls said LOVE all over the pages. I guess revisiting their cold, soulless generic yearbook entry was less harmful than being on the receiving end of their constant harping at me to lose weight when I was a teenager. Fatty they used to call me. Can you believe that? My own parents! Fatty! What was that scarlet tag supposed to do for my tenuous self-esteem?

Hearing me speak to myself, in a wild screaming rant, raging about those lovely parental memories, which are as alive today as they were when they actually spewed out of their sphincter mouths so many years, ago, the nurse called in one of the shrinks. Sitting on the edge of my bed, pretty upset, staring at the ceiling vents, Dr. T came in and sat down beside me. She asked me some questions in a sweet, clinically trained tone, which I refused to answer. Who was she? What did I know about her? Suppose I was part of some study? Who gave her permission to include me in the results? I turned the tables on her and asked her a few personal questions of my own, which she refused to answer. So, we had a Mexican standoff. The quietness got boring after awhile so to make it interesting I told her I was changing my name to 7-UP. Why, she asked. Don't you remember that commercial? It was a classic. She did not remember. She lives in a cocoon. I gave her a few hints. I told her how I am the *un*cared for, *un*appreciated, *un*hugged, *un*minded, the *un*loved. "Oh," she exclaimed, "the UNCOLA!" Bingo! That was work. She says to me, "Let's talk about this." We already did, I decided.

Granted the wine business is open to ridicule for anyone not in the know. That is expected and understandable. I mean, who wants to drink something that tastes like an oak tree? I get it. However, I know what is legitimate, what is real. I cannot claim humility at the altar of my knowledge, because that would be false humility. I cannot say this is the *honest truth* since that is a sure sign that all the words I have spoken prior to that trite statement were neither the *honest truth* nor anything that even resembled basic truth. Therefore, I will just say it. I know what I am doing. I spent eight years of graduate study, and intensive on the ground 'in the vineyard' study learning the vagaries of the business, the nuances of wine growth and production as well as the realistic possibilities for what makes for greatness in a glass of wine. Therefore, I know the full meaning of what is theoretical turned into reality when it comes to terroir, oenology, and bio-dynamism. I know how to precisely match the soil, grapes and viticulture. I know how to help yield merlots that are lush and round, nuanced and fine-grained. It is within my ability to discern which vintages are superb, elegant and tense, with aromas of violets and sweet tannins. In France, I worked with eleven different types of soils. I can distinguish why one particular merlot is far superior to any other because it was superbly adapted to a certain region's rich clay and gravel soils. My knowledge is not of the mile wide and inch deep variety. I do not need to excel at vinous Trivial Pursuit although I would win the game every time. My knowledge, wrought with hammer and anvil, is broad and deep. I have worked with some soils that come from the foothills and have experience with the very stony, slightly rounded edges of limestone or marl, dolomite, quartzite and slate, the highly permeable soils that allow the water to seep into the deeper layers of clay. I can taste the wine and know it is perfumed with flowers, citrus, and has a smoky, sandalwood scent. All the fancy notes attributed to specific wines are not phony words, not idle words to me. They are real words that have real meaning. I know all there is to know about winemaking.

All the knowledge I acquired, and all the experience, do they die with me? Does my life mean nothing? Is it not more than simply passing along information to another individual or a corporation? Am I not instead, sending it out into the world; is it not more than what someone has written that can be checked out at the local library. Can it possibly be a spiritual thing? Do I not send my spirit into the world while I am still alive, when I am still in my body? What I did not know enough of, unfortunately, was man's base nature, the greedy, crude, unbridled core venality, the self-aggrandizing side of the male species in this business, manifested no more prominently than in the souls or dark cavities that take the place of souls, within my one of my new employers. Barth wants to use what I know and what I can do, but James wants to corrupt it, exploit it to the point that it is ugly and diseased like some of their present mildewed rotted vines. He wants to destroy what I spent my adult life learning. He is less dignified than the rich soil encrusted beneath my fingernails. That is why I naturally gravitated to Barth, who is passionate about the art of winemaking.

I know a lot. Then, again, I know nothing. There are times that I know I want to die. Like right now for instance. Men. I've had a few. Most of them disappointments. Except one. Claude. In France. A gentleman, courteous, kind, sweet, handsome, passionate, considerate lover, married, just not to me. He made me feel desired for the first time in my life. Although his wife was certainly a stunning French model he saw another side to beauty in me that transcended the physical realm. Yet there is the trust issue. I sorely resented that he never told me he had a wife.

Of all the negative experiences in my life, other than my parents' willful neglect of my needs as a child and adolescent, the crushing deceit by Claude rose to the top of my list. After I debased myself in a paroxysm of tears one day in response to years of malignant parental cruelty, which gave my parents some kind of perverse vindictive satisfaction for their efforts, I thought I made an ironbound decision to never again demonstrate even the slightest emotional vulnerability before another human being. Of course it happened again upon receiving the devastating news from Claude. This time I swore I would never again visit that mythical land of love and romance, to which I likened to returning to a charming cottage in the forest, only to find a gas station in its place.

After I somewhat recovered from that tragic and painful fiasco, I shut down completely, built a steel girder defense around my heart to prevent it from ever opening again, even in the slightest. I poured myself into my profession, but that only served to reveal the gaping hole in my heart, the tenuous fragility of my spirit. I got depressed. I got manic. I did something that spun me off the rails, that put me back on that 28-day cycle. No, not the menstrual cycle. The 28-day average tour in the psych ward cycle. I apparently need the Thorazine to blunt the psychosis. The splicing of the soul episodes occur less frequently now, so I can avoid the longer continuing institutional care stays, yet the episodes still come unannounced at the worst possible times. For me. For B&J. Yet, because they are uncharacteristically patient with me so they can extract so much of my soul, I decide to cooperate with everyone on this tour of the Easthaven vineyards. I will answer Dr. T's innocuous questions, without being a smartass. I will behave. I will not be the head nut in the nuthouse as Dr. A so unprofessionally describes me. I want out of here. I will take my meds. I promise.

At first glance, the first impression so to speak, is not what I am particularly good at. You know, the whole discernment thing. On paper, the arrangement looked good. Barth was the brother with wine in his blood, and vines for his veins and ventricles. Even in this maritime climate, even in sandy, glacial soils he was able to cultivate and occasionally produce exceptional wines, courageously growing some exotic varieties, such as lagrein, teroldego, blaufrankisch, and goldmuskateller, all pure, delicious, energetic and alive. He achieved unprecedented success for the region in that elite restaurants up and down the east coast served B&J wines. When this phenomenon occurred there was much celebration and favorable press coverage but as it turns out, it was an anomaly, an exceptional season not since repeated, as B&J reverted back to mediocre status. Consistency accrues to greatness. Besides the wine coursing through Barth's blood, so was bloodlust running by capillary motion through parallel channels inside his mind and body. Yes, Barth had a thing for the ladies. Any lady. Sometimes, even his wife. But most especially, any lady who worked for B&J Vineyards. No one was safe. It was only a matter of time before he came after me. He preyed upon any individual who had a heart beating beneath ample breasts and a vagina. I do not deceive myself for a moment thinking he saw me as Claude once did. As I sat at my desk one sunny August afternoon, I felt his hot, exhaust pipe foul breath streaming down upon my neck. His heavy cologne did not obscure his musk smell, all his hormones worked up for a new conquest. But I let out with a scream, the pitch and shrill of which quite common in the psych ward, but otherworldly outside of it, so much so that it became one that he never experienced before in his puerile, lascivious life. He turned tail and ran out of my office and never propositioned me again.

Other than creating a rather bothersome afternoon for me, I did like Barth. His redeeming quality is his passion for winemaking, the noteworthy, admirable, envious search for a mid nineties Robert M. Parker, Jr. rating. Yet, he did not live long after that unpleasant encounter. I was only working at the vineyard a little over one year when he gave up his spirit. Now stuck with the business side of the equation, I am obligated solely to his big brother, James. Not ever one to mourn the loss of anyone who did not genuflect before the altar of his ego, James was somewhat less than elegant when he described the circumstances of his brother's death. Yes, he would invariably say, Barth died of a massive coronary, but doing what he loved the most, caught *in flagrante delicto* with his red-hot new secretary, Maria Consuela, who did not know the difference between a keyboard and a key and a board. But, boy oh boy, could she ... you get the idea.

James is very presentable, very smart and very cunning. He needs a new partner, now that his brother is gone to the great vineyard in the sky. Does he conduct a search? No. Vet potential investors? No. Solicit the services of headhunters who specialize in our industry? No. Does he make a Faustian pact with the most corrupt zoning appeals board supervisor on the east coast? Yes! A man disaffectionately known as the Ghost. He is called the Ghost by nature of his physical appearance and by his evil-spirit inspired work habits. The Ghost is a tall man, extremely thin, with strands of wispy white hair blowing in various directions on top of a narrow, egg shaped head. His lips are pencil drawn on a pale face, tiny, pin-backed ears, a proboscis worthy of its own museum, sitting below a set of steely gray, beady eyes. He just appears at times, out of nowhere, slithering into a room on the quietest feet, as if wearing only socks rather than shoes, appearing suddenly and stealthily behind his latest vineyard owner victim, with ominous clipboard in hand. He is a man who does not believe in making appointments. The Ghost simply shows up. And written on that fearsome clipboard is a laundry list of violations that only he can make disappear.

Over the years, B&J has paid the Ghost off handsomely, along with every other vintner in the region. The Ghost drives a Range Rover. The Ghost lives with his cats in a hacienda style house high on the bluff overlooking the sea. Everyone knows he is on the take. Yet, he covers his tracks very well. He is not alone on the Zoning Board of Appeals, but, as chairman, he has significant sway over all the other ZBA sycophants. He is reviled, despised and the recipient of numerous death threats. Is it his power that attracted James?

That is part of it. What James found most appealing about the Ghost is not what havoc he creates for anyone wishing to do business within his vile and corrupt realm. It is the secret of the Ghost's heart, what he covets more than anything else in the world that put him at the top of a very short list. The Ghost greatly desires to be in the wine business himself, a wannabe who yearns to be a player. Even with all the graft he accumulates during the course of the year, it would never be enough to go into full partnership with B&J. Money is not what James needs, however. It is what services that only the Ghost can provide to further James' master plan for his vineyard that was his free ticket to a limited partnership. It is that same master plan that turned my stomach inside out and should have sent me running to apply for a position at the nearest peach orchard. It is that same master plan that left a few dead bodies entangled in the vines one late winter day at B&J vineyards.

As it turns out, I signed up for something that turned out to be quite the opposite of what I expected. I was not the power broker I naively imagined myself to be. Not in this situation. My education and experience in the wine business meant something when Barth was still alive. Pervert that he was, notwithstanding, he supported my career and shared my vision for the importation of the finest French clones that would make the difference between a winery that had LIVE MUSIC TODAY with hordes of get a buzz at little cost partygoers spilling out of the limos and buses to guzzle bad wine and listen to old folk singers dispassionately droning tried and true recognizable tunes, to a winery that consistently produces great wines. To his credit, Barth never succumbed to making money from the mob. He and I opted for class, not only in wine cultivation and production, but to its presentation as well.

Barth put me in charge of the installation of an high grade camouflaged speaker system that would stream classical music up and down the vineyard rows as customers strolled along on tours, enjoying the fresh air and sunshine while learning all about viticulture. He insisted that I take charge of the music selections as well. Soft chamber music for the light whites, perhaps some *Sturm und Drang* Wagnerian pieces for the deeper reds. In theory, and by design, the vines would speak to each individual passing by, placing her in an ethereal trance like state, more apt to sip than gulp by the time she reached the tasting room. We wanted a vineyard that would not only be the envy of the region, standing in sharp contrast to all the run of the mill competitors. We would gain a reputation for supreme excellence on the national, if not international stage. But it would take time and Barth knew that and was willing to invest the time it would take to accomplish it, of course not knowing what little time he had left on this side of heaven or hell.

James had no plans to wait for Father Time to make an old man of him before he reached his primary goal. He must have been planning his grand scheme even before his brother passed. He left little time for mourning the loss of his younger sibling and business partner before he set the wheels in motion, barely waiting ten days after the funeral before he broached the subject with the bureaucratic hack known as the Ghost. He did not even consult with me about the intended collusion with the master denier of variances and supreme collector of bribes for quick turnaround decisions. James' level of sleaze on a business level was higher than his dearly departed brother's ability to keep his zipper zippered. I could have moved on, even to an established Napa winery. Several of my contacts at UC Davis and the West Coast wineries kept in touch with me, sometimes hinting not too subtly how I downgraded my resume by taking the assignment at B&J. Anything on the east coast was laughable. The California snobs unashamedly professed their judgment confidently and rightly so at the time. I still had smoking pipe dreams of vinous grandeur on the east coast. My chimera, however, was quickly glissading down a slippery slope. Something stopped me from being outraged. Hubris? Arrogance? More likely, it was a combination of my guilt and gratitude because the brothers kept me on with no loss of pay despite my various untimely visits to the hospital. Also factored in was my desire to see the plan through, the original plan of exquisite vine cloning of French plants that was the basis for my hiring in the first place.

I knew I had to make my move before I would be left to shrivel up and die on the side of the road like a diseased black rot cutting. I needed in on the deal between James and the Ghost. With Barth gone, these two schemers would be lost without me. Who else but me had the contacts in France to make the right selection of cuttings? Who else knew the rules of the U.S. and State Departments of Agriculture regarding the necessity of quarantine and disease prevention as well as the challenges on the other end, presented by the Establissement National Technique pour l'Amelioration de la Viticulture (ENTAV). We had to be patient. The rewards would be manifold. There were no shortcuts. Barth bought into that principle. His brother did not.

The original plan that I put together with Barth and James, with mostly Barth's enthusiastic endorsement, was far removed from the new plan that James and the Ghost were hatching behind my back. Again, I had my spies out there who told me enough to prepare myself for the inevitable confrontation. I reassured the workers that if anything ever happened to these two clowns, I would take care of them. The greed exhibited by James and the Ghost was exceeded only by their stupidity.

What I had originally proposed to do and both owners had agreed to, granted one owner was more enthusiastic than the other, was to find and select the vine cuttings and produce vine clones, genetic variants of grape varieties that have been developed and propagated to emphasize specific characteristics. My tour of Chateau Haut-Brion introduced me to the program of clonal research already in play at UC Davis. Yes, we could import clones from France but the plants would have to go through quarantine and testing to ensure they were not diseased. That would take up to two years, with no guarantee of how many plants would survive and we might end up with just a few vines that would need to be planted as source material for buds to graft on to rootstock. Plant the vines in spring, and by the third year, you might have something. Theoretically, this would produce more buds and the whole process could take up to ten years. Foundation Plant Materials Service at UC Davis advised me how to import French rootstocks licensed by ENTAV. I was geared up to put the ten-year plan into motion but I needed to first safeguard my future in light of what the two tricksters were doing behind the scenes.

A good friend put me in touch with a local attorney, a first generation Irish charmer who could throw the shite further than anyone I ever met, and had a pitbull tenacity when it came to negotiation. The Irish esquire convinced me to chip in a sizeable portion of my dear old Mom and Dad inheritance to qualify as a limited partner so that my contribution was more concrete than abstract expertise and academic credentials. By the way, I believed that I got the inheritance by default. I entertained the thought that maybe my parents felt guilty after all those years of malignant indifference and the imposition of psychological abuse, namely played out by the ruthless name-calling of their only child. The truth of the matter was probably more mundane. They were never ones for charitable causes. They guarded their money selfishly. Their stinginess gave them satisfaction. I was merely the only one in line to benefit from the fruits of the their pernicious miserly lifestyle.

The Ghost was smart enough to do the same at the advice of his own attorney who convinced him that his unique, localized brand of corrupt influence would not hold up in court, if it ever came to that juncture. In fact, it might even get him into trouble he was told. His stake was equal to mine as he was able to make withdrawals from his graft account, subsequently refilling it by ratcheting up his efforts to extort more and even steeper under the table payoffs from the vineyard owners who had already been squeezed drier than the last glob of toothpaste out of a Colgate tube. As a result, he added exponentially to his already considerable list of mortal enemies.

I should have known that there was trouble ahead in my first meeting with Barth and James, which took place virtually the moment I stepped off the plane at JFK. Having the same conversation several times since, I remember laying out the whole process of clonal importation before them including how much time it might take to yield positive results. James did not realize how contorted his face became when he learned of the plan's daunting time frame. Any amateur student of body language could read James' unmistakable posture as one of pure agony. He tried to keep a professional poker face, but his right eye twitched every time I added another year to the previous sentence. During the entire meeting, he kept clenching his fists, unaware I studied his every move.

Despite the trauma of Barth's death coupled with the appearance of the Ghost, I held it all together mentally. Sometimes it's the little things that derail me psychologically, albeit that there is no such thing as a 'little' thing for a mostly incurable mental patient such as myself. I do not even recall what set me off, forcing the last few stays at the hospital, but they were probably little compared to the unfortunate circumstances unfolding before me at present. This was a big thing, worse than I ever imagined. Maybe I can handle the big things. I made sure I took my meds and kept my weekly appointment with the psychiatrist. Yet, when I met the Ghost for the first time, I thought I was ready to commit myself to Easthaven for an extended stay.

When James introduced him to me, the Ghost said nothing, staring at me with his beady eyes, immediately extending his hand, not giving me enough time to say oh I just put lotion on or any old excuse to avoid grasping what turned out to be an unpleasant, dangling, limp, dirty, damp dishcloth of a handshake. As I stared back at those soulless eyes, I felt the need to wash my hands with bleach. I believe he and I communicated to each other a wordless and mutual disdain. James asked me to tutor him on some of the finer, more nuanced aspects of the wine business so I was obligated to spend more time with him than I thought my stomach would allow. He did not know the wine business. He only knew how to ruin the business for naïve and uninitiated vineyard owners.

He showed up, always without prior warning, with documentation that the tasting room was on land solely zoned for agricultural output, and neither the newly built fermentation cellar nor the salesroom met the specific setback requirements and so on. He always waited until the structures were built before he laid down the hammer in order to extract the maximum liters of blood for each infraction. Woe to the owner who did not bother to hire one of the Ghost's expert cronies to guide them through the tortuous permits process, authored by none other than himself. The Ghost just waited in the wings, the unseen evil spirit lurking behind a gauze scrim. He always arrived with a clipboard full of violations. He was truly ignorant about the wine business despite deriving a substantial second income from the region's owners. He did not know the difference between a fine Bordeaux and a jug of Five Star Twister. His beverage of choice was a cup of hot water flavored with a wedge of lemon. Despite all this, James knew the Ghost lusted to be part owner of a vibrant, up and coming winery. The Ghost's life was drab, lonely and grim. Life as a bona fide vintner would add color and verve. Just the glamour of it all thrilled him.

What made the situation worse, after those meetings I was forced to have with the Ghost, I came to know more than James about the Ghost's ulterior motives and they did not favor James. The Ghost had a plan all his own which would be the undoing of them both. After a short period of time, listening in on their scheme, I was often confused about which man was the devil and who was the devil's apprentice. I soon found out how unequivocally they deserved each other. Rather than feed off each other, as was their original scheme, they devoured each other. And, the egregious misjudgment made by one of them manifested itself as the ultimate undoing of both of them.

If I had the option of being an independent observer I might have enjoyed the spectacle. They kept me out of their devious, private discussions, yet I knew a lot of what was going on. Little busy bee vineyard workers who had an allegiance to me would gossip about guaranteed overheard conversations on a regular basis. I had to be careful, however, to avoid staying around too long if they were going to engage in any criminal activity. I made sure not to leave a paper or email trail. Aside from signing a legal contract outlining my rights, duties and obligations as a limited partner, which was all legally binding and court approved, I stayed out of harm's way in terms of getting involved in any of their shady activities. I never offered my opinion in response to any vineyard worker gossip. I literally kept my nose clean, instead saving its sensory power for the pleasure of sniffing the fine bouquet wafting from the bottle of *Domaine Leroy Richebourg Grand Cru* I brought back from Cote de Nuits, France.

I kept my own counsel but actually started to think that I could benefit from their crookedness and ill-fated plans to conquer the world of fine wines. It would be a stretch but I began to convince myself that all crooks are stupid to the extent that they have a tendency to overlook the distinct possibility concerning the imposition of unknown plans simultaneously made by other entities that become barriers thrown in the way of even the most meticulously designed plot. We have all read the book or have seen the movie about the bank robbers who, for months, plan the perfect theft of an armored truck that always arrives at a certain street corner in the city at a very specific time every Thursday morning. The crooks launch numerous trial runs, time everything down to the last second, only to see their unsinkable plan thwarted when, on the fateful day of glorious riches, the armored truck takes an unexpected detour around a utility vehicle blocking a vital street because of a gas leak. Who could have predicted this occurrence on the very day?

It was close to the end of winter dormancy. On the first warm day after an especially harsh storm pelted the entire region with rain, sleet and snow, the workers started to drag the mowers, pruners, compost spreaders and other seasonal tools and equipment out of the sheds to get them tuned up and ready to spruce up the grounds in advance of another ho hum season at B&J Vineyards. Another group of workers tested the sound system for the Classical Walk through the Vineyard.

The melting snow dripped off the eaves of every building throughout the day, sounding as if the last storm never ended. One of the workers, nicknamed the Giant, did most of the heavy lifting. A huge six foot five inch specimen with a mass of natural muscles not artificially manufactured in a gym, liked to show off his brute strength during the season and on occasion would entertain the patrons by lifting huge wine casks off the ground onto his shoulders. The Giant was also on the alert whenever an unruly male customer consumed too much vino for his own good and needed to be escorted off the premises. Once an especially belligerent misbehaving macho man resented the Giant's initially polite entreaties and took a swing at the big man. Amused, the Giant did not flinch and let the man's blow land on his massive chest. The force of the man's swing did not move the big man one inch but the resulting recoil sent the drunken customer hurtling to the ground. It was quite an amusing spectacle.

While all this activity was taking place, other workers were giving me daily reports on the nature of the escalating arguments taking place between James and the Ghost. Each day for the last several months the screams and the curses got louder and more personal. The principal antagonists got so focused on their dislike for each other, they no longer cared whether or not they argued behind closed doors or in full view of the staff. Without bringing the other limited partner, that would be me, into the heart of their vitriolic disagreements, they discussed their differing views of B & J Vineyards' future. It was never that they wanted to spare me the unpleasantness of it all in any sense of compassion or consideration for my sensitivities, because I represented to them the exact opposite of what is the only issue the two of them agreed upon, taking an unsavory and ethically challenged, if not illegal, expedient shortcut to stardom in the world of winemaking. They had scuttled my long-range plan for clonal regeneration many moons earlier. They dismissed it immediately upon the hearing of it. They were solely interested in the enterprise of clonal smuggling. Without involving me, they conspired. Without being given the chance to express my dire warnings of the potential risks they were about to expose themselves to, they planned to go full steam forward with the implementation of their risky scheme.

At first, their disagreements centered on who was concocting the most implausible and least viable plan. One wanted to smuggle clones out of France by ship, bypassing both the French and the American authorities. Another plan involved purchasing already vetted cuttings from a Canadian supplier and smuggling them across the U.S. border by truck. Over the course of the winter months, they each developed the starry eyed, unstoppable lust for power. They were drug dealers, but instead of cocaine, their drug of choice was lust for the world's finest wood for planting the next crop of Merlots. The prize for greed tipped favorably toward James' suggestion. He intended to forswear stopping at the cuttings, adding transportation of soil as well by ship container loads through the portals of a porous Mexico, paying all the necessary bribes along the way. They never for a moment in their bloodlust search for power and prestige in the wine business stopped for a moment to consider the depth to which their inane plans had devolved to. Who would float the next impossible idea? The canning of transplanted Bordeaux air?

The prospect of long-term prison sentences never occurred to either one of them. Until one seminal day in their short history as partners in crime, James threatened to expose all the untoward deeds actuated by the Ghost that could be documented by the corroboration of every other vineyard owner in the region. To counter this ominous threat, the Ghost matched James with a promise to subjugate the principle owner to a freight train full of violations that would push B&J Vineyards into bankruptcy, leaving the eighty-four acres fallow and subject it to inattention for years so it would again become the hard scrabble property it once was before all this wine madness started. Then the Ghost would buy the abandoned property at a distressed price once the sure to happen bankruptcy auction took place. That was just his midterm plan. Needless to say, they each reached the point of no return in their acrimony. Their hatred for one another reached epic proportions. The vituperative insults and threats were too personal and cutting for there to be any return to civility. They surely reached the point of extreme hatred for one another. Deceit met greed. Fury met rage.

For a fleeting moment, James mourned the loss of his brother, Barth. Despite his shortcomings, he would have brought some sanity to the current situation. On the other hand, if he were still alive, there never would have been the devil's pact made with the Ghost. The lawyers would soon be called in to begin the process of litigation. The end was near. At first, I watched this unfolding in horror, then in amusement.

There were a few days of peace when neither James nor the Ghost made their appearance at the vineyard. The workers, relieved from the never-ending volatile and tense atmosphere, were finally able to go about their duties peacefully. On the third day of this welcome yet unexpected calm, I sent the workers home an hour early and decided to finish my work, such as it was with an uncertain future ahead of me, in the comfort of my cottage. I did not see the Giant but I am sure he was somewhere on the vineyard pulling dead trees out of the ground with his bare hands.

I sat at my desk before the window overlooking the cove and enjoyed the carefree, wild plunges the buffleheads made to find food in the shallow water. The swan couple joined them in their graceful necking and preening as they too dipped into the water in order to find sustenance on the murky bottom. Then, the peace was suddenly interrupted with the sound of a distant gunshot. I paid it no mind, as the vintners had free license to shoot any hungry deer desperately searching for food after such a harsh winter. Every winery stored a shotgun or two on the premises. I am sure we had one ourselves, in one of the sheds. I hated to see anything that had a beating heart felled into a lump of flesh on the ground. Sometimes uninvited thoughts flooded my brain, swelling up in me actually with the disturbingly provocative notion that I would rather see the shooter of those beating hearts fall to the ground instead. See how that feels, dying in your new spring LL Bean outdoorsman outfit. But that does not make any sense, does it? Even those shooting bastards have a heart and a brain, I think.

The shot did set me off I have to admit. I felt the unmistakable wave of another episode speeding toward me, a Niagara Falls rush with only one unstoppable goal in mind, a destiny-driven push over the edge. Sometimes I deliberately keep a pebble in my shoe, and walk around all day with that annoyance so that I would feel alive at every moment. Now I am feeling somewhat dead. I have to protect myself. I cannot spend another menstrual cycle in the psych ward. I have too much at stake and too much to do while these two idiots try to destroy everything around them. The rush to the edge is powerful so I decide to encase myself inside a block of marble.

Since I am entombed irretrievably inside, I cannot chip myself free. I would prefer that Michelangelo come along and chisel away everything that is not me or Rodin if the Italian is not available. While I am safe inside I can make preparations for what I will tell Dr. T just in case someone drags me out of here. I will make sense this time.

I will not manufacture imaginary cruelties perpetrated by my innocent parents. I will tell her what I truly know, deep inside. This way she can write on her report that I do have a grasp of reality, that I do know the difference between delusional incoherent fantasies and the concrete reality of what is before me, around me and inside of me. I will tell her what I know. And what do I know better than the wine business?

Before the sculptor chips me out of my protective block of marble, before anyone sees how desperate I am as I bloody my hands clawing out of the stone cage by myself, I will tell her what I know. I will start by telling her whether she is a collector and traditionalist or a more adventurous drinker about the discovery-driven reports from the ground and tasting room which wines boast pedigree and style and details about the region's unique terroir she might not fully understand all the terms but it will come across as real and reveal to her important things about every style and price point how to order wine in an elegant restaurant that pairs gourmet meals with classic French pours she might ask me as I teach her about the difference between a vineyard and a winery so she would be forced to rethink her traditional notions and even be jealous about my vinous future and how significant it is for our region such as it is to return to indigenous grapes and not to worry about quantity but focus on quality in this potentially great wine-producing region she and I live in will no longer be marred by bulk grape-juice production formerly used to bolster blends everywhere instead focus on cutting yields and local varieties and steer away from the international grape craze when vast amounts of Chardonnay Cabernet Sauvignon and Merlot were planted for centuries and get with the shift to indigenous grape varieties that produce incredibly drinkable fruit-forward wines and whatever grape will take root in the clay and limestone soil and wait patiently for the well-mannered reds that offer a wealth of dark berry flavors and earthy gamy notes and delight when they take on a fresher profile and display a vibrant red-cherry color wild strawberry and herb-crushed flavors and softly structured tannic profile similar to a flashy California transplant Zinfandel named for its ability to ripen early a juicy rich wine with spicy dark berry and violet tones giving it more lift and levity while tannic when young it will soften with age eventually becoming supple and finessed and concentrated in dark fruit tones complex leather and sweet spice characters creating the opportunity to boast varietal bottlings that show off its crisp clean fruit tones laser-like acidity and stony minerality all made possible from a vineyard developed from its cuttings nurtured by a vineyard manager's (that would be *moi*) best friend steady winds and sunny days are here again as we have a history of becoming the state's first AVA proudly to be an American Viticultural Area humbly starting out with twenty some odd varietals and clones now there are approximately 1,350 wine grapes in the whole entire world yet almost 75% of wine is made from just eighteen grapes many of which are adjudicated by wine's single biggest influential gatekeeper Robert M. Parker, Jr. I am surprised no one has unloaded a shotgun on him as yet but he will die out even before he dies because the whole industry is undergoing a massive sea change and the influence of a certain type of serious wine critic is on the downward spiral attention wine drinkers everywhere be on the lookout for the next hotbed of indigenous grapes harvested by hand withstanding strong winds and a hot sun and little rainfall which contributes to their intense character a vigneron did this not a moron capable of leaving a grape on the vine until it is shriveled by the sun creating an intense red fruit to nutty (there's that word again) and oxidized that's me nutty and oxidized bottled in a demijohn then covered with wicker a little different than my current encasement in a massive block of Carrera marble sitting in a strange corner of a Burgundy terroir Oh the Horror Oh the Terroir trying to capture a unique sense of place you know it when you taste it as it is alive, mutable and singular (I am singular but still single unfortunately) any winery worth its licking salt will produce at least one single-site wine again worth repeating that you can make a difference by resisting the big bucks temptation to become a cheap bulk wine producer and trade that in by establishing a reputation as a well-respected producer of quality wine replete with lemon curds apple and delicate florals wreathed by a prickly palate in its mineral expression or if you prefer a silky savory earthly expression of a complex muscular and tightly wound (like me) grape begging to be cellared (lock me up!) a truly gluggable and lubberble red that appeals to our younger wine enthusiasts I am not a fan of anyone who corrupts these youngins like they corrupt the land we are talking about New World sustainability focused on the environment but not entirely ignoring the social and economic realities of grape growing think about it for a minute how many millions of wine drinkers would gratefully without hesitation abandon any number of utterly delicious irresistible wines panting for the stem glass in their private cellars and switch to wines that taste like piss because they originate from vineyards that have adopted sustainable practices an intentional effort at producing wines based on organics and biodynamics just think about the czars of sustainability are here to stay in the cooler damper oceanic climate where wines have a style both more mineral and more crisp than whatever you are familiar with such as the right terroir for Pinot Noir (that's a poem by the way) mixed with clay and chalk in warmer parcels again ripe with red cherries and dark plums laced with red-cherry acidity not considered a grand cru variety where only a fraction of the plantings are responsible for unique white wines planted in great sites deliberately lowered yields giving voice to their full potential with a closed nose with hints of cherry purity treating the palate to a follow-up of an equal balance of the finest pure cherry firm tannin bright freshness graced with just a little dark peony scent understated and full-bodied but wunnerful wunnerful elegant growing on you slowly like a subtle rash now full-blown disease scented with hints of cinnamon and oak meant only for the luminous palate with insistent freshness and the purity of ripe dark cherry with ample magnetic and seductive depth (like when Claude and I made magic together in bed) the same pure fruit of a relationship that tingles you know where with romantic and aromatic echoes of cherry pepper and licorice all shimmering together on the lightness of our bodies we want to be approachable mind you priced somewhere in the $10-$15 range expressing overt, ripe red and black fruit aromas and flavors thanks to you Dr. T working together on this hot sunny day which will contribute to the ripeness and lush flavor of my mental health the only flavor I need on cooler nights which enable the grapes of my wrath to retain their acidity and freshness. There, I said it all in one breath. She will know, professional that she is, I am making progress.

Then, I hear a second shot and a third shot, surely on our premises now, coupled with our speakers vigorously sending out the intense sound waves of Camille Saint Saens Samson and Delilah *Bacchanale*. I love that music but I did not choose it for our Classic Walk through the Vineyard. It was too fast-paced for the intended leisurely, educational stroll. This selection by Eugene Ormandy's Philadelphia Orchestra is more chase than walk music. A lull in the music. Time to reload.

As best I could figure out, the Ghost had scheduled an appointment to meet James at the office so they could settle their differences. James thought for sure the Ghost would bring along his shyster lawyer, an unsavory sort, yet one who was a perfect sleaze match for this particular client. Rather than being accompanied by his attorney, however, the Ghost came instead with his best friend, his beloved Purdey twelve-gauge double-barreled shotgun. He knew the town police were accustomed to gunfire at all different times of the day and night which left him unconcerned about their possible intrusion upon his hunting expedition. The Ghost snuck up on James without warning and pointed his shotgun at the startled owner, standing near his desk. James turned tail and ran out the back door, fearing for his life. So he should.

For the moment St. Saens' *Baccanale* faded in the background and, strangely, jarringly was replaced in my brain with the Johnny Horton hit, *The Battle of New Orleans* that my father incessantly sang just to rankle my nerves when I was a sensitive teenager. For spite of the old bastard's memory I adapted the lyrics of the only song he knew to what I visualized in my head: *He fired his gun and the owner kept a-runnin'/There wasn't nigh as much time as there was a while ago/The Ghost fired once more and James continued runnin'/On down the Chardonnay through the vines of Teroldego/Yeah James ran through the briers and ran through the brambles/And he ran through the bushes where a rabbit couldn't go/He ran so fast The Ghost couldn't catch him/On down the burgundy to the row of sweet Merlot/He fired once more ...* Just then, as the Ghost was wont to do, he slipped quietly around the row of James's favorite Riesling wood, and spotted the principle owner of B&J Vineyards, panting, out of breath, vomiting profusely onto an unpruned vine. The Ghost pulled the lever and pumped an ample multitude of buckshot into the back of his hunted adversary. James fell forward into his own vomit, an ignominious end to a once promising future as the owner of at least a minimum Robert M. Parker, Jr. 92 rating.

The Ghost did not bother to reload, his mind for the moment relieved of any wrongdoing in what he considered to be a justifiable homicide, uncovering the extent to which he remained delusional. As he bent over to retrieve the spent shell casings just a few feet from the body of his former partner, blood still leaking into the spring softened firmament, a two hundred pound lump of dead flesh now ready for the compost heap, he felt the sudden and painful pressure of a punch to the middle of his back, as if hit by a large rock shot out of a cannon. The Ghost fell to the earth with his head landing between two plants. His unseen attacker placed one huge hand around his neck and with the other gave him a few smart, forceful whacks to the back of his head, knocking him nearly unconscious. As he lay there, the music selection suddenly shifted to Haydn's oratorio The Creation (Die Schopfung), not only one of my favorites but one that brought back such pleasant memories of my graduate days at the university. It was an exquisite recording, one I treasured with all my heart as it was a gift given to me by a close friend at graduation, a double CD set with libretto of the memorable performance at my alma mater, which I attended and swooned over for many weeks afterwards. What I distinctly heard was the angelic singing of the University Chorus in concert with the UC Davis Symphony Orchestra: Jeffrey Thomas, conductor; Suzanne Karpov, soprano (the angel, Gabriel, Eve); Nils Brown, tenor (the angel Uriel); Thomas Meglioranza, baritone (the angel Raphael).

As the Ghost lay dying, the right side of his face smothered flush upon the earth, his syrupy left eye left open to see close up the coming of spring and to experience with each one of his senses this long-awaited season of growth when the vineyard truly comes alive and beats with a resuscitated heart. That was all he had to depend upon at this stage, his senses, for the force of the blow immobilized him to the point where not even his fingers twitched. His left nostril took in all the flavors of the good plantings. He was one with the strands of good purslane, clover and plantain weeds, his mouth drooling a mix of blood and spittle, his left ear ligated with an errant vine, so soon creeping out of the dead winter earth. Death can be so beautiful and forgiving at times.

In his last moments, for his listening pleasure, the angel Gabriel whispered softly the Recitative *Genesis: Chapter 1, verse 11* "And God said: Let the earth bring forth grass, the herb-yielding seed, and the tree yielding fruit after his kind, whose seed is in itself upon the earth; and it was so." Though handicapped with only the left side of his face functional, because of the drama and intensity of these final moments, he received the fullness of touch, taste, smell, and sight of the usually ignored elements of life at the doorstep leading to eternal life. He could not recall ever knowing the sensory earth so intimately as he was presently forced to smell it. He never knew there existed such an infinite variety of tiny insects that now crawled from the syrup of his eye to the drool of his mouth. Not to be minimized was the fact he was fully cognizant that each one of those biting insects would outlive him, some even drawing sustenance from his flesh and blood. His vision, now blurry, saw close up the early bugs of spring, a few of them crawling over his cheek and half closed eyelid. Here in this trench, he, like so many before him facing the liminal moment between life and death, with great effort, spiritually climbed out of the atheistic foxhole of his non beliefs to at last embrace the early Christian teachings instilled in him so many years ago in Sunday School just as he heard a sweet angelic voice implore him "Let the earth open her womb." Who would dare judge him now? Certainly, there were gradations of his sins amply committed over the years and he realized in these final desperate moments that he was presently inclined on the steepest grade of his unfortunate life. For so many years he thrived within the confines of his livelihood on ruining lives but just moments earlier he actually took a life. His life now hung in the balance, or rather lay flat on the ground.

The whole experience of being entangled in the vines he never before appreciated much less understood, brought him back to a Bible passage he learned in Sunday School so many years ago. Yes, it was the last chapter in the Book of Jonah. With his spirit as damaged as his broken back, he recalled "The Lord God appointed a bush and made it come up over Jonah, to give shade over his head, to save him from his discomfort; so Jonah was very happy about the bush. But when dawn came up the next day, God appointed a worm that attacked the bush, so that it withered." Then, in the last moment as he prepared to give up his spirit, stepping further along the unavoidable approach to the altar of his long abandoned childhood faith, he strived to remember the comforting words of a beautiful John Henry Newman prayer about the shade being drawn at the end of the day, the shadows lengthening, the troublous life, the hush of a busy world, and then something about the fever of life being over and our work being finished. Also, something about peace, peace at the last came to his mind as the mighty fist of his attacker hammered home the death blow against the back of his egg-shaped skull.

It is clear to me that in these troublesome moments I live inside my head. But now my only wish is to decapitate myself as I am being boiled in a clear plastic bag for the entire world to see. I am totally disembodied. My body no longer exists in its original form. It has no form at all. It is not intact, inhabiting a closed environment such as within a thin shell, an egg where a slimy (with afterbirth fluids being licked off by the mother) little duck would soon emerge and seek warmth beneath her mother's breast. My eyes, ears, bits of brain, heart, kidney and other tiny parts of me float in a creamy, mucous mix, like so many bits of corn, potatoes, baby shrimp, and onions. Then, the disconnected parts of me are put on the burner, still sealed in the bag, cooked over ultra-high heat, confined and close, yet some parts that should be in close proximity to one another being drawn further apart, making it infinitely more difficult for me to retrieve them and put them back in place, to become the fullness of who I am.

The earth did not open her womb for me. There is no relief from the knowledge I do not wish to know, not that I am falling apart, but that I have indeed already fallen apart, cut open, not born, but poured out into the fire, filth and dust. I am sick. Very sick.

<u>The Pizza Parlor, present time</u>

That was O.G.'s story, as best I remember her telling me. With the TV screen showing a professional European soccer match, of interest to the six, young Italian guys working the oven, spinning the dough, shoving slices of pizza on paper plates across the counter, the boss making change at the register and another kid folding boxes, I keep my eye on her, at a safe distance. She keeps her eyes focused on the front door, as if waiting for a friend who is late. It is almost noon. In just a few minutes the parlor will fill up with locals looking to have a slice or two and a Coke. O.G. has been here for at least twenty minutes, waiting. The boss won't be too happy with her taking up a whole booth, preventing paying customers from finding a seat.

I then see what was so remarkable about her appearance. In between passing bodies, I notice that she does look quite different than when I last saw her. No more pockmarked skin although I find it hard to believe that she is med-free. An identifiable figure, adorned with a dress hugging a slim waist in between full breasts and hips. Wearing jewelry, not the costume variety as far as I could see, but well appointed and a tad out of place in a local pizza joint. She has the unmistakable look of prosperity, nails spa-refined, skin restored to a soft, feminine glow, a beautiful face with cosmetics delicately applied revealing a rosy blush, quite a dramatic change from psychotropic body-altering medicine, bearing all the telltale signs of a woman who has power, not merely dominion over self but a certain confidence that rises to the level of self-assurance, well-earned and by the way, purified through a furnace as hot as the parlor's brick oven, a soul that is tossed and flipped many times over until it is sizzling hot.

As the customers file in, I see one of them head towards O.G.'s booth. She does not get up to greet him but motions that he should take a seat. He is such a big, broad man, his girth depriving him of any choice but to sit on the very end of the bench, opposite O.G., necessitating the extension of his left foot into the aisle as he is unable to squeeze between the edge of the bolted-to-the-floor seat and stationary table. Although I did not get a good look at his face, I see that he is dressed in a suit and jacket that did not hide any part of his muscular physique, no tie but a form-fitting expensive purple silk shirt, with the top three buttons undone descending from his thick neck showcasing a forest of his chest hair, nesting a masculine chatelaine of serious Italian bling. Just a quick observation caused me to think he must be a mobster, with a name like Fat Tony, for example, except there was not an ounce of fat on his body. He said a few words to O.G., then stood up, snapped his fingers and motioned to the fellows at the counter to change the channel on the TV, which broadcast soccer 24/7 in that place. The counterman said, "What kind of paisano are you? You don't like football?" The big man gave him a long look and the worker quickly grabbed the remote and turned off the TV.

I began to feel that O.G. was in danger sitting opposite this imposing, sinister giant of a man. Part of me wanted to slip out of there, ignoring her. Then, I would never be happy with myself for being such a coward. I walked over to the booth where O.G. and the big guy sat. I thought for sure he would have something to say to me and that O.G. would be glad I showed up. But when I got closer, virtually right in front of her eyes, she looked right past me as if we never met. Perhaps she did not want to be reminded of our times together at Easthaven. It has been awhile since we last saw each other. I'm sure I look different to her, much thinner now and almost totally bald. She started talking to the man, not in the least bit afraid of him, it seemed to me. I tried to catch his attention, putting my face close to his, but he paid me no mind, being totally engaged with O.G. I then walked through the crowd of new customers and disappeared into the world of wine, music, and a soft breeze that carried barely visible particles of pollen and dust from one nose to the next. Ah, Spring!

THE CENSUS TAKER

Clipboard in hand, with forms to be filled and boxes to be checked, seasoned New York census official, Paul Ostrander, hiked deep into the woods to record data about the occupants of a simple log cabin at the southern edge of Pine Meadow Lake. The remote Callaghan homestead was his last call in the village of Sloatsburg. Over the years, Carney Callaghan had added a few rooms to the original structure that dated back to Colonial times when Carney's ancestor, a veteran of George Washington's army, bought the property from the Chief of the Ramapough Lenape Nation.

Ostrander took pride in meticulously recording birthdate, education, occupation, income and other vital information for each household. Accuracy meant everything to him. One more knock on the door and he was done with this assignment.

Carney opened the cabin door and scrutinized the civil servant dressed in a suit and tie. Ostrander handed his card to the mountain man, barefoot, shirtless, hair askew, wearing loose-fitting coveralls.

"Minnie Mae," Carney said to his wife, "Come here a minute, will ya. We got a visitor. He gave me a card ya gotta read."

"We don't git many visitors here, Mr. Ostrander," Minnie Mae said, "I got some nice vegetable soup on the stove. Why don't you join us fer lunch."

"Not sure I can stay for lunch but thank you anyway," Ostrander said.

"What are yer doin' in the middle of the woods?" Carney said.

"I'm here on official business for the New York Census Bureau."

"Now you *have* to stay fer lunch. When Minnie Mae invites'em in nobody ever goes away hungry 'n she kin answer all your questions." Carney put his big hand on Paul's back and guided him to the wood plank table. Minnie Mae gave the soup a stir.

Ostrander explained the purpose of the 1905 Census and assured them he wouldn't take up too much of their time. Minnie Mae answered the man's questions, cleaned off the table, excused herself and headed over to the barn, leaving Carney alone with the official.

"Going back to your sons, Mr. Callaghan ..." Paul said, his pen and clipboard at the ready.

"Call me Carney. We et a meal together. We're friends now."

"That's very thoughtful of you, Carney. I have to say that was the best vegetable soup I've ever eaten."

"Can I call you Paul??

"Sure," Paul said, shaking Carney's hand, "Minnie Mae was very helpful but I still have a few questions about your sons. Did I hear her right when she said your eldest son's name is Ox?

"Yeah, Ox. That's what she said. Ox's chopping a cord of wood so he kin store it'n sell fer charcoal. If ya decide to stay fer dinner you'll meet him in the flesh. Don't sit next to him 'cause he'll eat his'n yours. He's a growing boy."

"Is Ox his given name?"

"Sure is. Minnie Mae give it to him a coupla years ago. A local farmer had one of his cows fall into a ditch'n my son volunteered to pull'er out."

"Was he able to?"

"Nah. He shoulda jumped inta the ditch'n git under the animal. But his brains ain't fully formed yet. Patrick is the smart one. But Mickey …"

"Who's Mickey?" the man said, looking at what he previously wrote.

"My son."

"You have a third son?"

"No, his name was Mickey before he tried to help that farmer. But when Minnie Mae'n I saw how strong he wuz we renamed him Ox. Anyhow, back to the story. He pulled that tail right off that cow. Right off his ass. But if he'd git under it in the first place, the cow'd still have a tail." Carney looked out the window and saw Minnie Mae carrying a pail of feed for the hogs. He turned to the official and said, "Where wuz I?"

"The cow … the tail … and …"

"Oh yeah. So Ox tries to put a big patch on the cow's bleedin' ass. Minnie Mae thought that wuz stupid so she took my big musket'n tried to put the sorry cow out if its misery. She explained to Ox who was close to cryin' what it'd be like if a cow dint have a tail to swat flies away. How would you like it I sez to him, if those stingin' flies were pickin' at yer clinker dingleberries all day? Ox felt bad fer a few seconds but never had much of an attention span I suppose that's not a bad thing. He don't dwell on the bad stuff too long which is a good thing."

"Did that really happen?"

"Sure did. You can walk a coupla miles north off the main road'n see the herd of Jerseys at Jonseys Farm. You'll see a cow with no tail. It's a tourist attraction now. The other cows stay clear of her cuz she's different, ya know. Cows're funny that way. Not nice sometimes. They give ya milk when you squeeze their teats, and then some sass when they're so inclined."

"I thought you said your wife shot the cow?"

"Well, Minnie Mae's not used to handlin' a big musket like that. She wound up shootin' a snake on the ground 'cause that's as high as she could lift it. At least she got somethin' fer her trouble."

"So Michael ..."

"Who's Michael?" Carney said.

"Wouldn't that be Mickey's Christian name?" Mr. Ostrander said.

"How'd ya know we wuz Christian? Most Chinese aren't Christian. Until the missionaries git a hold of us. Anyhow, for yer purposes his name is Mickey'n that's how we're gonna baptize him. He's the only kid in the family ain't been baptized yet."

"Why is that?"

"Ox is bigger 'n stronger than me now'n it's gonna take a few of us, plus my injin grandkids who are gittin' bigger'n stronger every day to hold Ox under til he sez he loves Jesus."

"How will you know if he's under water?"

"I read the bubbles when they's under water. Three bubbles in a row is a yes. Works every time. We baptized all the other kids in the Yankees river. We call it that now since we converted to Chinese. But Ox said he ain't ready to accept Jesus. He wants to keep sinnin' for a while longer before he makes up his mind. That's his plan but Minnie Mae'n me got our own plan. When the preacher man comes around, the two of us will get Ox drunk'n drag him to the river'n convince him time's runnin' out on him."

"You have a priest that comes around?"

"He ain't Catholic but he's some kind of minister. He goes by Reverend Dooze. He's a carpenter down there in Sloatsburg'n doin' me ministerin' on the side. He ain't got much teeth left but he sure can preach. Tells us all 'bout the Bible'n Jesus. Patrick likes him a whole lot. Every time he comes around, Patrick asks him to teach him another coupla words in the big book he carries. He knows Greek words'n Hebrew words too. Nice man."

"Who's Patrick?"

"Tail. Patrick's tail. Once Minnie Mae'n me made it official to name Mickey Ox, she thought it proper to name Patrick Tail, as Patrick wound up holdin' the poor cow's lost tail after Ox got pissed off'n threw it at him."

"Can you tell me about Minnie Mae. I just need to know her age, education and so on," Paul said.

"Okay, now we're talkin'," Carney said, "Another man at the mill had an interest in Minnie Mae but she figured he wuz just looking for a woman to have commerce with - ya know, just 'nother woman to fuck is how she put it ... and it just so happens she wuz lookin' 'round the mill herself at the same time. She also met a smelter, a miner'n a logger in town yet lucky fer me she wuz attracted to a mountain man. That wuz me. She splained the diffrence. Those other men are varmits, she said I ain't droppin' my draws for none of them. Minnie Mae told me that I was an animal too but more the domestic kind, like a dog, a cat, or a ... by the way, do you count ghosts on yer form there?"

"Never," Ostrander said.

"How'bout body parts of different folks?" Carney said, lifting his hand to show Paul the missing half of one finger on his left hand, "One day I git a little careless in the machine shop. I hardly felt it til I saw blood pourin' out'n this fingertip of mine layin' on the floor. I tell you it's strange seein' a part of yourself when it ain't attached to your self where nature originally intended. So I asked some of the workers if they could try to put the tip back best they could 'n cauterize it. Damn, they tried but they ain't no doctors. There was no whiskey around 'cause the boss dint allows it so I jes bit the bullit'n yelled like Minnie Mae when she's poppin out 'nother puppy. That hurt somethin' mean 'n the burnin' flesh stunk real lousy. Anyhows, it stung worse than stickin' yer hands in a nest of angry bees – but the damn thing still fell off so I took the little fella home in a bag 'n went to bury it in the field. I mean it wuz part of me 'n I missed it. That's when I discovered other bones 'n parts of humans buried in that general area. Not too deep so some of them parts of skeletons surfaced 'n just lay on that part of the field I never paid much mind to. That's what I meant when I asked 'bout ghosts. Maybe I wuz delirious 'cause I wuz lightheaded from losin' so much blood I guess 'n I saw the ghosts was dancin' like Ezekiel's bones. Do you know your Old Testament, Paul?"

"Not as well as I should." Paul said.

"I betcha yer hear a lot of tales from folk in your travels," Carney said. Bet ya could write a book."

"Maybe I will some day. The cow's tail is the best I've heard so far," Paul said.

"Aw, you're trickin' me now, aren't ya?" Carney said as he put his arm around Paul's shoulder.

Paul did stay for dinner and met Ox and Tail. They are big mountain men like their dad. Minnie Mae had to slap their hands with a spatula several times when they tried to grab all the bread off the tray. Paul went home thinking it's one thing to check boxes. It's a whole other thing to meet a family like the Callaghans.

Hopewell Junction

He stood there blowing hot air. What a loudmouth bloviator I thought. He must have been born with a mini bullhorn organically grafted onto his larynx. Judging by his volume, the audience he hoped for was everyone in the waiting room. From what I observed from my seat opposite his, no one was listening except the elderly couple sitting right next to him. They were stuck real good, boxed in with no other seats to be had. It was late at night. The trains ran but once an hour. He wasn't saying anything threatening to them. If you took away the loud voice and analyzed what he was saying, the subject matter was actually kind of interesting. Not interesting to me and by the looks on the older couples' near dead faces, there was little interest on their part. But someone somewhere could have been interested. Who knows? Every now and then, the woman would look directly at him and give him one of those painful half smiles out of politeness, I guess. He never once asked them a question about themselves. It was all about him.

I came in the middle of his oration and so at first I thought those older folks were his relatives or even parents. He was going on and on about a cousin coming in from Colorado. He was going to show her the town because she's never been. But then I fell asleep for a few minutes and when I woke up, I swear there was a different older couple sitting in the exact same seats as the first pair and Mr. Self-Importance was still discoursing on his life and still waiting on his cousin from Colorado. Anyway what he said next really threw me because I didn't know what the hell he was talking about. Therefore, I'm going to pull the curtain back a little bit, so to speak, and let you listen in on him yourselves as if you were sitting in the station, having just missed a train home and stuck right where I was with this windbag pontificating *ad nauseum*.

"I teach ESL because I have a gift for languages. I lived in China for several years and spent about six years in the Czech Republic. Travelled throughout Europe and Asia. Lived in Russia and India for a while. Some of the African dialects are tricky but after you live with the natives for a while you can pick them up somewhat." At this moment the little old lady leaned toward him as if to get in a word or two, if he would only shut up for two seconds. I don't know if the old man heard a word he said because he just stared straight ahead with somewhat of a half smile on his face. I don't know who or what he was looking at, if anything. Certainly not at me. Not anyone behind me or to the sides of me. The waiting room was packed. If he was staring at the wall there was nothing to look at except industrial gray paint and cheap aluminum molding. There was a map on the wall that looked kind of interesting but he wasn't staring at that. I made a mental note to look at the map myself later on, once I could figure this guy out.

Anyhow, the lady almost fell on the floor, leaning over her husband, to get this guy to shut up for two seconds. He finally noticed her and this is what she said, "We were in Denver once. It was late at night and a big storm came in and they were about to shut the airport down but we got the last plane out of there. I've never slept in an airport before and I never plan to."

That being said by the lady, the orator gives her a slight nod and jumps right back into what he was saying before the interruption: "My cousin should be coming in from Denver very soon. Anyhow, like I said I know many languages. I speak Korea fluently; a little Japanese, Italian … Italian is the most beautiful spoken language. With all the open vowels and how one word just flows into the next like a smooth, not too thick syrup being poured from one container to the next with nothing spilling over – just a nice, easy flow. Each word a poem. A thing of beauty. Something to linger on and savor. Whereas Japanese is an ugly language. It is harsh. That's all I got to say about that. But I speak it. I'd probably be able to speak it a little bit more if I didn't hate it so much. I'm not saying I hate the Japanese people. Don't get me wrong. I just don't like their language. Like I said I speak a lot of Korea, probably because I lived there for so many years."

The guy stood up but continued to blow and blow from a standing position. Did you notice that twice he said, "I speak Korea?" And the lady never corrected him. It's like if I said to someone, "I speak America or I speak Canada," the whole chorus of the full waiting room would have said hey stupid, America and Canada are countries, not languages. If he's got a gift for languages, how come he couldn't get that right?

Anyhow I had enough of this guy and went over to look at the station map. As I walked past him, he didn't smell so good and his boots were scuffed. His jacket was too thin for this kind of weather and his hair was all matted down and there were deep lines cut into his dirty, sunburnt face that I hadn't noticed at first. What do I care? I'm just killing time in the waiting room. I walked over to look at the map on the far wall, stepping over some outstretched legs and around cranky kids who were up way past their bedtimes. Maybe their parents took them to some show, which they cared less about and would never remember anyway. What a waste of money. They should have saved their dough and their time and just stayed home where it's warm. A lot of people underestimate that simple pleasure. Staying home where it's nice and warm.

In any event I got a close look at the map. I could see the date it was published at the bottom right hand corner and man was this in need of an update. It was brown with age and parts of it peeled back from the frame but there was nothing else to look at. Despite the map's age I was fascinated by the many lines thrusting out from the center of the city, spiking into all these different communities I never even knew existed, much less visited. The surface of it looked like the vein pattern on a slightly cracked egg – random, uneven and going seemingly nowhere and everywhere at the same time. The perspective of the lines made it seem like some of them got thinner, disappearing into the point of infinity like they teach you in art class. By the way it was an electric map. Not all the bulbs worked but I guess the original intention was for the train passenger to see at a glance the progress of her train coming in and what stop it was currently at along the way. But mostly, the only bulbs left were the last stops on each line so you didn't know where the hell your train was or if it was stuck or derailed or whatever. I looked at the names of the stops. Some of them I recognized and some were just names of areas in various towns and villages: Pond Reserve; Ringgold; Two Daughters; Elderville; Bottom Green; Hopewell Junction. That has a nice ring to it.

Hopewell Junction. I hope everyone is well in Hopewell Junction.

It got quiet all of sudden. What I would call peace. The blowhard must've been resting his vocal chords for a few seconds. Even bloviators need to catch their breath so they can create the next imaginary moment of their pathetic lives. I turned around so I could see what he looked like with his mouth closed. He wasn't there and half the place emptied out. So I ran down the stairs and jumped into the first car I could, with the doors closing behind me. No more last call, all aboard. You're on your own in this city. The train had ten or twelve cars so it absorbed a lot of bodies. Only two or three other people were in my car as far as I could tell. I couldn't see everyone. Some people slump down and take up all four seats like it's their private slumber car or something. Probably so few people occupied this car because it had a bathroom. You'd think that at least one of the passengers would just pull the bathroom door shut as they came in so it wouldn't stink so much for them and everyone else. Piss on the floor. Piss all over the raised seat and toilet paper rolling on the floor. Some people are pigs. Their mamas never taught them bathroom manners. They're probably pigs at home too. But who wants to even go into a car like that? No, they'd rather just flop and go to sleep in three seconds, then miss their stop forty minutes later, call their wives and say could you pick me up at whatever the last stop was. So the wife would have to drive in her pajamas and bathrobe to pick the lazy bastard up. How some people stay married is beyond me. I shut the door, sat in the middle of the car and said to myself shut up. I'm going on and on just like the blowhard waiting for his cousin from Colorado, even if it's only in my mind that I'm ranting. I should just thank God for my blessings. Thank you God for giving me such a stinking life. Merry Christmas to you, too.

Anyhow, I'm glad I made the train. Usually, I like to get to a train a few minutes early. I like to walk the whole stretch of the platform so I could feel the hard bumps of the yellow rubber warning mat on the soles of my feet. It's like a free foot massage. I didn't even care where this train was going. If the weatherman was right for once it could be the last train out of the city tonight. And I needed to get the hell out of the city. I couldn't stand it anymore. Everything's going to shut down if the big storm they are predicting actually comes this way. A blizzard's coming, no two ways about it. I hate the way they report the weather these days. They give you the wind chill factor on top (or below) the actual temperature. Just give me the damn temperature, will you, just like they did in the old days. I'll figure out how cold I feel all by myself. They must need to rationalize their meteorological degrees or the big pay they get. That's the job I want, weatherman. That or a government economist. Either one would work for me. Right or wrong you still get paid. Best two jobs in America in my opinion.

As soon as the train came out of the tunnel I knew they were right this time. This would definitely be the last train tonight. The wind and snow just smacked that double thick glass and chased me to the outside seat. As soon as I switched to the aisle I couldn't believe my eyes. Here he comes, the blowhard, walking right toward me and it was too late to slink into oblivion. Maybe he's on the prowl for another old couple that can absorb one of his grandiose lectures.

Oh no! Too late. Eye contact made. He stands right

over me. I can see close up in the harsh light that his fingernails are long and filthy, as if he scraped grime off a car engine or worked with dirty machinery and never washed his hands. The skin of his face was his worst feature. Tanned, but not a healthy beach tan. A beaten by the wind tan. Too many lines and furrows. His hair was greased back but not handsome slick like Robert Redford in the *Great Gatsby*. This guy needed a good scrubbing. The dim light he had in the waiting room was his best friend.

"You got a ticket?" he said standing right above me. I could smell a trace of cheap booze on his breath.

"Why, you the conductor?" I challenged him. He didn't answer me right away but just stared at me. A penetrating, intimate stare. I didn't want to mess with this guy. He was big and looked like he didn't give a shit if he lived or died. I guessed that he'd fight to the death if he had to and for no good or noble reason.

"You got a ticket or not?" he demanded.

"No," I said, "I didn't have time to get one."

He takes a crumpled paper out of his pants pocket and hands it me. "This is a ten-tripper and it's got one trip left on it. It's for a different line, but that doesn't matter. They have to give you some credit based on zones," he said in a voice much lower than his waiting room voice. I took the ticket from his filthy hand. He left his hand extended so I could shake it. I thought he'd have a much stronger grip but I was surprised how soft and gentle it was. A caress almost.

"Where are you headed?" he wanted to know but I wasn't about to get personal with a stranger, so I just shrugged my shoulders. I only wished I could sprout wings and escape this tight trap but he might follow me from one car to the next. Like those two older couples in the waiting room, I was now his captive audience.

Instead of asking me again where I was headed he offered me some free advice. "Listen, we all got stories," he said in a whisper, looking down the aisle to see if the conductor was anywhere in sight. He then leans closer to me and his breath is a mix of wine, beer and smoke. "Don't get off at Hopewell Junction tonight. Just go to the end of the line."

"Why are you telling *me* this?" I asked but his stare shot right through me, "We all got stories buddy. You got a story. I got a story. My story is probably pretty close to yours. Had a job. Lost a job. Then the bitch kicked me out. Blah, blah, blah. What does it matter?"

"Why the end of the line?" I had to know. What's his reasoning? Then he started rocking a little bit. I thought he was going to fall right into my lap and I'd never get him off.

"Just go to the end of the line," he insisted, "Jimmy's the maintenance guy on duty tonight. He leaves the waiting stall open. And he keeps the heat on all night. I swear he's going to get fired soon but he's got a heart for guys like you and me."

"You and me?" I thought to myself, "So now we belong to the same club?"

"Jimmy isn't much of a janitor and the stall smells like piss but it's our piss, if you know what I mean," he says straight out, "Anyhow, what you can do is stay there all night and you'll be warm. If you see Jimmy, just tell him you met Butch."

Okay. Now the blowhard has an identity. His name is Butch. What kind of name is that for a professor of Italian, and some Chinese and Korea? He speaks Korea I reminded myself and that made me feel a little better about the company I was keeping.

"Why shouldn't I stop at Hopewell Junction?" I asked.

"It's locked up tight," Butch advised, "You'll freeze your ass off there. But you want to stop there in the morning."

"Why?" I had to know.

"Stay at the end of the line until the sun comes up. You'll want to get out of there before the commuters start to come in numbers. Someone'll complain and ruin it for Jimmy. Ruin it for Jimmy and you ruin it for the rest of us."

"The rest of us?" I inquired.

Butch didn't answer me but just took a deep breath and the breeze of all that wine, beer and smoke attacked my nostrils. Better than smelling salts and it lingers. I was no longer tired. I was into this guy's lecture. Now the wind really picks up and bangs against the window with a big, powerful fist. I could see the snow drifts building in a hurry.

Butch catches my eye, "This one's a killer."

"I hope not," is my answer, "Where are you getting off?

"Hopewell Junction." Before I could ask him why, he simply says, "I got some business there tonight, but you do as I tell you and you'll survive the night. Come back to Hopewell Junction in the a.m., a little past daybreak. Go down the escalator and speak to Steve. That's his sandwich truck you'll see at the base of the escalator. Go up to him and tell him Butch is your friend."

Now Butch is my friend. And I thought I just wanted to be alone tonight. Butch continues, "Don't go up to him if there are a lot of customers around. Wait until he's got a little bit of a lapse and make sure you mention my name. He'll give you a black coffee and a cheese danish. That'll hold you for a while. Later on I'll tell you what stations are good for a sandwich or soup or …" This time Butch did keel over. Right into the seats across the aisle. He got up almost immediately and looked straight ahead. He spoke quickly, "Listen. The conductor's on his way. Just give him the ticket I gave you. I got to move along but some other time I'll tell you which stations are good for food, washing up, pitching for money, all that good stuff you've got to get to know especially on nights like this."

"How are we supposed to meet up with each other?" I asked.

"Here's my business card" he laughs as he hands me an empty chewing gum wrapper from his pocket, "Just call me at my office and my secretary will tell you how to get a hold of me. Or call me on my cell. Better yet, email me. I always answer my emails." He looks down the aisle again and offers this last bit of advice, "Tomorrow when you come back from the end of the line the conductor on the six o'clock train is an idiot. Just tell him anything that pops into your head. What works best is you tell him you got beat up and the mugger took all of your money and your monthly pass. Got it?"

"Got it," I said as Butch left my side just as the conductor came into our car.

"We'll see each other again, don't worry about that," he said as he hurried into the next car. I called out to him, "Did your cousin from Colorado ever show up?"

"Nah. She owes me a lot. I don't expect to see her again as long as I live," he boomed in his waiting room voice.

The conductor took my ticket. No questions asked. I rode to the end of the line and slept where Butch told me to. As it turns out the storm wasn't as bad as they predicted. The sun was coming up and I could see down to the streets. The heavy salters and plows were chugging along one after the other, not meeting much resistance. It was freezing though and when I see Butch next, I'll ask him where I could get some gloves and maybe a heavy blanket.

I got off the train at Hopewell Junction and saw some commotion at the bottom of the escalator. As I rode down I could see the commuters using the up escalator as a staircase because it wasn't moving. They looked even unhappier than me. How bad could it be that they had to climb stairs. Lazy bastards. In a way I'm glad I'm not a commuter anymore.

As I got closer to the bottom, I saw the sandwich truck but there was a lady pouring the coffee, handing out donuts and making change. She didn't look like any kind of Steve to me. When I got to the bottom, I could see the up escalator making one false start after another, clicking and clucking in the rhythm of a big mechanical zipper stuck in hopeless monotony. People were all sorts of pissed off. No free ride this morning.

I could see there was something stuck in the bottom step of the escalator. A big piece of thick cloth all bunched up, mucking up the gears. Then, off to the side, I saw where the piece of cloth came from. People were stepping over what looked like the body of a man. The bare skin of his pale left leg was exposed to the freezing cold. There were traces of dried blood on his leg.

I walked around the sandwich cart to get a closer look at the body on the ground. The man wore a thin black vinyl jacket and cargo pants. The piece of cloth sticking in the gears of the escalator came right off that man's pants. I knew it was Butch but I didn't know if he was alive or dead.

"Where's Steve?" I asked the sandwich truck lady.

"Who's Steve?" she answered as she made change for a twenty.

"The guy who owns the sandwich truck," I said.

"I own this truck," the lady said defiantly, "You must be talking about the guy who used to have this route."

Now I'm getting a little excited as the commuters continue to step over Butch's body to catch their trains. "What about this guy on the ground? Anybody call for help?" I said.

"Listen buddy. I got a business to run," she said, "Besides that guy doesn't need any help right now."

"Why not?" I asked, wondering if this whole scene was real or some kind of cruel fantasy.

"He's gone," she said as another customer took her coffee and cheese danish and stepped over Butch.

Yet another customer came up to the lady and asked: "When's the mechanic coming to fix the escalator? Do you know?"

I knelt down to look at Butch. There was a pool of liquid that spilled out of his mouth. It iced up like a little skating rink beneath his dark face. One side of his face lay flat on the ground. His flesh sealed itself to the cement. Man and ground were one with each other.

The trains ran on time this morning. Steam floated out of each cup of hot chocolate and coffee. I suppose people got to their offices on time. I suppose that the heat came up from the boiler rooms in most of the office buildings. And surely there was an ample supply of liquid soap in the bathroom dispensers and back-up toilet paper in each one of the stalls. By the time I left Hopewell Junction, things were almost back to normal. Some kind of official vehicle loaded up Butch's body. I couldn't look to see how they got his face off the frozen ground. They put his big body in a plastic bag and that was it. The coffee lady had a good morning. Sales were strong.

If Butch were still around he could have told me about the Ringgold station. I wonder if that stop is good for anything. Now I have to find out for myself. What happened with all of Butch's knowledge, I wondered. All that knowledge of languages and whatever else he knew. Now that he's dead, does it go with him wherever he's headed? Is it packed tightly in his brain like a compressed file on a jump drive? What happens to all of that? Maybe the good news is that it stays with the people he taught. That's if what he told those old folks was actually true.

Seeing his body on the ground and a piece of his cargo pants stuck in the escalator wasn't the most pleasant sight I've ever beheld. I plan to fight to stay alive today and I have to admit I'm a little bit scared. Too bad Butch didn't live another day. I guess we could have been real friends. He had a lot more to tell me. I don't really know if he had all the language skills he bragged about or if he could even speak one word of Korea. But I do know two things for sure: the ticket he gave me was good and I didn't freeze to death last night. Most importantly he did teach me about the end of the line. He sent me to a place where I would be warm. At least for last night. Tonight's another story.

THE BAPTISM

The priest lived a relatively long life but for many of those years he was tormented by the nagging fear he would die a horrible death. Nothing in his life throughout that dark time supported this notion but in one of his more down in the dumps moments, he confessed to a fellow priest that it would be so profoundly twisted that after living a purposeful, at times genuinely righteous life that he would die in some ignominious manner, his end of life decided at the hands of some anonymous low-life who would drag him into a dark alley, stick a knife to his throat and demand his old wristwatch and the contents of his wallet which rarely contained more than twenty or thirty dollars. Upon realizing that the haul was considerably less than he imagined it would be in this pricey part of town, the vile thief would madly twist the knife into his heart in some inexplicable sense of street justice.

That is not the way he died, yet his eventual death was equally shameful. His desire for the way in which he would die was not so much a product of trying to be heroic but of hoping that he would go out of this ungrateful, dispirited world in a proverbial blaze of theological glory, perhaps a modest martyrdom of sorts, drawing his last breath in the service of salvation, guiding some poor soul to the clear path of grace filled redemption by demonstrating God's unconditional love, in a spiritual as well as a physical sense. He thought of this often and was determined for it to be so. His priest confidant suggested he focus his attention on the poor in spirit as well as the poor in material wealth and not worry so much about the endgame.

Jesse Cairo could hear footsteps behind him as he sat in the third pew, awaiting the start of the Funeral Mass for Father John. He turned his head slightly and saw an elderly woman perform a perfunctory half genuflect at the paschal candle, then proceed directly to the Virgin Mary's altar.

She bowed before the statue, knelt down, made the sign of the cross, stood up and dropped a coin into the slot at the base of the rack of candles. It was obvious the coin had little company in the cashbox, as the singular sound of the coin dropping to the base of the metal box was the only noticeable sound in the cavernous sanctuary. She lit a candle and as she rose, she blessed herself again quickly and returned to her pew in the far reaches of the once thriving church. Just moments later, Jesse turned his head as before to witness a second elderly woman perform the exact ritual. Moments after that, as the second woman headed toward her seat, yet a third woman enacted the identical routine.

The three older ladies lived much and lost much in their many years, but did not share their lives with one another. Jesse turned completely around and observed that the three women sat far apart from each other, each working their rosary beads, with heads solemnly lowered, bony knees firmly locked together, pressed upon the kneeler. They attended the seven a.m. Mass every morning as well as all special masses that had communion on the program, including the Funeral Mass that was just about to begin. Whether they knew the deceased priest was doubtful, as Father John was never assigned to this particular parish.

Other than the church ladies and Jesse, there were three other people in attendance for the Funeral. Jesse assumed they were related to Father John, cousins from out of town perhaps. The man, woman and young girl sat in the front pew across the center aisle from Jesse. As the celebrant priest entered the altar area through a side door, he headed directly to greet the family seated up front. The man started to rise, but the priest put his hand on the man's shoulder, allowing him to remain seated. Jesse noted, that although seated, the man could look straight into the priest's eyes without so much as stretching his neck an inch.

At the beginning of the Mass, the priest swung the thurible, murmuring incantations, blessing the casket. The aroma of incense, while pleasant to most, sent one of the old ladies into a coughing fit. She left the sanctuary. On the way out, she dipped two fingers into the holy water basin near the door, blessed herself and left the building.

Communion was offered to the family and the two remaining elderly ladies. Jesse passed on partaking of the Eucharist. As the ladies returned to their seats, they cast subtle looks at Jesse over their cupped hands. Jesse made eye contact with each one and returned each one of their stares with a pleasant smile.

The priest spoke kind words about the deceased. Jesse listened intently, and determined that the officiating priest never knew the former priest being buried today, whose body lies within the unadorned coffin. The celebrant read the epistle and the Gospel with due reverence, sprinkled holy water upon the casket's white pall, reminding the faithful of the hope promised at the occasion of their own

Baptisms, though most had no recollection of its occurrence as they would have been just a few months old at the time.

When the service came to an end, the family up front arose. The man, dressed in a gray sealskin greatcoat, with a vented shoulder cape, stood up first, rising as in sections to his full height, just a few inches shy of seven feet. He stepped aside to allow the woman, seemingly half his height, and the girl nearly as tall as the adult woman, to walk in front of him.

The funeral home's pallbearers wheeled the pop-up church truck bearing the coffin through the narthex, down the marble steps and loaded the casket into the hearse with the church truck collapsed beneath it. The priest greeted the family of three and Jesse as they left the church. Jesse shook the priest's hand and asked him if he knew the connection between the family of three and the deceased. The incurious priest shrugged and said that he had no idea.

The two remaining church ladies stayed in their pews, blessing themselves repeatedly. No announcement was made concerning the trip to the cemetery but Jesse followed in his Ford Ranger pickup, with hazard lights blinking. He followed the hearse and black limousine for some forty odd minutes, until the vehicles stopped near a bench along the side of the road, just short of the Route 94 underpass. The drivers of the two vehicles and the tall man unloaded the church cart, propped it upright, and placed the coffin on top. The church truck was situated adjacent to the bench with the wheels locked in place. The drivers got back into their vehicles, made a U-turn and headed back in the direction from which they came. The man, woman, and the girl, holding a fast food restaurant paper bag on her lap, sat close to each other on the bench.

Jesse assumed for a moment that this was some kind of transfer point and that another transport would soon arrive. The man undid the bottom button of his greatcoat, and meticulously picked miniscule pieces of lint off his slacks, then folded his hands upon his lap. He appeared to be as fastidious in his sartorial splendor as a younger, much taller version of the very crisp and precise Karl Lagerfeld. While the man made sure his slacks were without imperfections, his wife attended to the back of his greatcoat, searching for any evidence of dust or stray pieces of lint and picked them off as she spotted them. The girl put the paper sack aside and performed the same service for the woman, finding and destroying whatever strange particles appeared on the overcoat.

Jesse observed this wordless ritual for fifteen minutes. It reminded him of a *National Geographic* photo he once saw of a pack of grooming Barbary macaques. He diverted his gaze for a moment, looking in the direction of the horizontal crease where the underpass meets the sloping concrete footing. This part of the structure arcs from street level up to the underside of the highway, forming a narrow platform where the overhead highway supports a constant drumbeat of rumbling tractor trailers, buses and cars travelling at breakneck speeds. He saw, in this protected space, what appeared to be a makeshift homeless shelter, its blue tarp shield shivering with each passing truck, draped alongside a random assortment of milk crates, supermarket carts and piles of green contractor bags.

After what seemed like too long of an embarrassingly mute span of time, Jesse decided to break the silence. He got out of his truck, crossed the road and stood about eight feet in front of the man, saying, "I can take you to the cemetery." The three groomers looked past him to some distant point on the horizon. Jesse continued, saying to the man, "You can sit up front with me. There are two pullout seats for the ladies. The coffin will fit in the bed. No problem." No response was forthcoming from any of the three. After a moment, Jesse noticed something moving against the tarp, bulging in spots, most likely a body poking around in earnest. Still no response from anyone in this tight-knit family. Not one to give up easily, although annoyed, he spoke again in as helpful a voice as he could manage, "I can take you to Gate of Heaven or Valhalla. They're both over the rise there," he said, pointing, "Along the river bluff. Maybe twenty or thirty minutes from here. Max. Which one is it? I know the way to both."

Jesse sensed the man was not interested in the things of this world yet Jesse was bursting to reveal certain truths in order to dispense them into the world *he* inhabited.

The tall man turned his head momentarily. A sudden audible rustling noise on the ledge above caught his attention. He looked up. Jesse's eyes followed the same visual path as both men studied the activity taking place on the ledge as the blue tarp was now being drawn aside.

Remembering a saying on a greeting card once given to him by his girlfriend, 'You've never been ignored until you've been ignored by a cat', Jesse decided he needed to establish himself more strongly in the presence of these felines. "Look," he said, "I was subpoenaed by the District Attorney of Ramsey County to testify at Father John's trial. I put my hand on the Bible and told the truth."

At the mention of the word 'truth' the man looked intently at Jesse, staring into his eyes for an awkward five seconds. In the next moment, a human figure emerged from the highway shelter, a heavily bearded man dressed in torn, dirt-caked clothes. The homeless man waved to the people on the bench who waved in return. The tall man again turned his attention to Jesse, who spoke haltingly, "I … I identified myself in the court, told them of my relationship with Father and answered the attorney's questions as best I could."

As the homeless man rummaged through his crates, the seated man again started picking dust particles off his trousers and the females robotically joined in the grooming routine. Jesse returned to his truck and moved it on the shoulder, to get out of the way of the occasional car that travelled by on the rural road.

Before he ever thought of joining the priesthood, John LeBarron took a church organized pilgrimage to Rio de Janeiro, Brazil to visit the Christ the Redeemer statue at Corcovado. Like everyone else on the journey, he was awestruck by its beauty but that wave of enthusiasm could not outweigh his discouragement at having to contend with the crowds forming at the large number of gift shops at the base of the mountain, which sold an infinite variety of Christ the Redeemer T-shirts, flip flops, refrigerator magnets, bookmarks, mugs and infant onesies.

There was a more humble monument back in the States that moved him spiritually and sealed his destiny for the priesthood. He was made acutely aware of his calling on a different kind of pilgrimage, a basely secular one to Atlantic City, New Jersey. In fact, he rarely missed any of the weekend bus junkets from St. Paul to Atlantic City. The modest forty-dollar fare was reimbursed soon after boarding, with the reward of a roll of quarters, unlimited drinks, two meals and snacks.

After spending most of the day at one of the hotel casinos, mindlessly feeding coins into the slots, pulling levers, consuming free drinks offered by the cheery cocktail waitresses, he took a stroll on the boardwalk, grabbed a bacon and egg sandwich and walked aimlessly down several side streets until he spotted a concrete bench beneath a large elm tree in the courtyard of a church. He drank some of his coffee and took a few bites out of the sandwich and felt drawn to a statue of Christ very unlike the imposing one he saw on the mountaintop in Brazil. He was inspired by the subtle imposition of the statue's holiness and humility. It stood life size just a few feet from the bench. It was the figure of Jesus Christ with a sparrow on his head, another on his outstretched finger, and a third one lying on its side at the base of the statue. It was an unusual sight, in that he was accustomed to seeing statues of St. Francis interacting with birds and animals. He noticed the details, especially the birds' eyes. There were tiny black bead eyes embedded in each bird's head. Could they be onyx? Or ebony? Not quite bearing the awesome splendor of the Christ the Redeemer in Rio, Jesse was overwhelmed by the artist's attention to detail.

There was a pine board at the base, bearing words carved in English, Spanish, and Chinese, possibly appealing to the different ethnic groups who frequented this gaming town. It stated, "Seventy times seven I forgive you. If God so loves the sparrow, how much more does he love you?" As a young man in his early twenties, he gave up his gambling trips to Atlantic City and applied to the seminary within his hometown in the Archdiocese of St Paul and Minneapolis.

Jesse opened up to the tall man on the bench and told

him the following story: " I was in my last year of elementary school. I don't even remember how we met but one of the first things he asked me – he was in seminary then - if I wanted to go swimming with him and some other boys. It was winter and he said he was a member of the Y and they had a specific time on Saturdays which was set aside for young boys, just like myself."

Jesse hesitated, making sure the tall man was paying attention. The woman and girl turned their gazes upon each other, trying not to intrude upon this part of the conversation. Assured the man was listening intently, maintaining eye contact, Jesse continued, "I thought that was odd because I had just met him. He singled me out for some reason, I never thought about swimming in wintertime, only in summer, in one of the lakes. But then it got even stranger when he said, quite matter-of-fact, that I could choose to wear a bathing suit or nothing at all. It made me feel uncomfortable, yet on the other hand, he said it in such a natural way, that I didn't feel threatened."

On the night Father John died, he sat at the neighborhood all-male bar, as a defrocked priest, convicted felon and regular patron of cranberry juice mixed with two shots of vodka. Once a week, he brought a supply of a special brand of unsweetened juice to the bar. The bartender kept it refrigerated for him. Recently released from prison, having served one third of his original sentence, there was little reason to celebrate. His reputation had been ruined. He had no fight left in him. That is why he told his attorney he wanted the trial to stop so he could plead guilty to the charges against him.

At the time Father John admitted his guilt, the newspapers quoted the Ramsey County District Attorney as saying: "Typically defendants aren't going to plead guilty once the trial is already under way, but this is what this particular defendant did. He expressed great remorse about putting his accusers and their families through this ordeal and said he took full responsibility for his actions." The D.A. further stated that the Archdiocese of St Paul and Minneapolis responded quickly to the allegations. The Archdiocese released a statement that said it "deeply regrets the pain inflicted by a member of the clergy."

By the time he finished two of the cocktails, and was working on his third, two men in their forties entered the bar and sat on either side of the former priest. One of the men, dark-haired, tall, with a trim physique, put his arm around John and, with his free hand, picked up the cranberry vodka cocktail, sniffed it and pushed it along the bar to his friend's waiting hand. The shorter man, balding, with a faint hint of red hair, also smelled it and said to John: "What the hell are you drinking, Padre?"

"Do I know you gentlemen?" John asked, a little bleary-eyed.

"I wouldn't exactly say we're gentlemen. Let's just say we're still boys at heart," muttered the dark-haired man.

"Then who are you?" John asked, slurring his words. The shorter man laughed, moving closer to John, "Remember Mrs. Duffy?"

"I don't think I do," John answered.

The other friend moved closer, whispering, "She was the Irish biddy. The bitch the three of us paid back one early morning some years ago."

"The three of us? Paid back?"

The bartender came over to check on the new customers. The shorter man asked if he could order a tall glass of Manischewitz Concord Grape. As the bartender arched his eyebrow, the two buddies laughed and ordered two beers instead. A faint hint of recognition started to seep into John's alcohol impaired brain. He finished his cranberry concoction in one big gulp.

The trim man continued the story, "Of course the three of us. We planned it in the sacristy before the seven a.m. Mass. C'mon, you gotta remember that. It was a classic."

Seeing that John was struggling to bring that occasion to the front of his memory bank, the balding man filled in the blanks. "Mrs. Duffy, the Irish bitch. The meanest witch in all of St. Paul. She took communion every single morning. You gotta remember that time we sent her flying."

"Flying?" John said.

"Man, when we came up to you with the water and wine, you skipped the water altogether, then forcefully guided my hand to the other cruet. Together, you and me just emptied that consecrated cruet of Manischewitz into the chalice. A Saint Kilian's special - cheap kosher wine - Classic! You always had the best taste," pointing to his friend, he said, "Your turn."

"Like every morning, you were half in the bag by seven twenty. When you and I walked along the communion railing, nigh approaching the fat, stuffy and fully pious Mrs. Duffy you gave me the clue and I knew what to do ... according to the plan we all made before Mass. I was holding the paten right against her throat. You winked as you placed the host on her swollen tongue. I rubbed my foot as hard as I could on the carpet and the sound of that tsk tsk was music to my ears."

"That bitch reeled backwards and fell on her fat ass," added the other altar boy, "I wish we had a video of that."

The two friends, laughing so hard, were incapable of putting complete sentences together, sputtering their beer all over John's jacket, who remained silent throughout the episode. Starting to sober up, he remembered, not so much that particular event with Mrs. Duffy, but began to envision the two men as twelve-year old acolytes in their angelic cassocks and surplices.

"No one came to help that biddy. She just lay there. Her skirt was half way up her thighs. You could see the thick hose rolled up to mid calf, not making it past her varicose veins," patting John heartily on the back, he maneuvered his face so he could be nose-to-nose, saying, "We never lost stride. I was proud of you, Father. We just kept on truckin' along that rail and let her lay where she fell, moaning like a sick cow. Not one of the other altar rail biters came to her assistance. She laid there a good two minutes before the custodian came over. It was his job to clean the garbage off the floor."

John pushed away from the bar, trying to get down from the stool, but his foot missed the bottom rung. The men pushed him back up. "Let's go to the pool," one of them suggested.

"What pool?"

"The pool table in the back," the other one whispered, nearly kissing the ex-priest's ear.

"I don't know that game," John protested, feeling the sweat run down his sides, now fully aware of the danger lurking within such close proximity. He could smell the hot breath of both men, blowing at him from either side.

"We'll teach you. It's the perfect game," the taller man

said, his face turning into an insistent grimace, "It's got nice long sticks and hard balls. By the way, one of those balls has your number on it. All played on a table with soft holes everywhere. "

The short man grabbed the front of John's shirt, "And a sacrifice altar made of green felt."

Jesse's mother was impressed with Father John, though he was not yet ordained. On the day of her son's graduation from St. Kilian's, he came to the apartment and presented a gift to his protégé. It was a black hardcover book, slightly smaller than a missal, with gilt lettering: *The Imitation of Christ*, by Thomas a Kempis. Still a seminarian, but wearing simulated priestly garb, he inscribed it to Jesse: *What you do for the least of these, you do for me. Congratulations, John LeBarron.* The gift brought tears to the mother's eyes. Jesse still treasures the small book.

The homeless man came down from his ledge and spoke loudly to the family of three, "You've come to the transfer point, Zach. Soon you will cross the border." The woman nudged the girl who stood up and handed the bag she was holding to the homeless man. He grabbed it and opened it quickly, devouring the sandwich it contained in three voracious bites.

When Zach stood up, the whoosh of his sealskin greatcoat could be heard by Jesse, sitting in his truck. The tall man turned his head skywards, the shoulder cape broadening his shoulders even wider, raising both arms to full extension. When he spoke, the words sounded deep and throaty, rising and reverberating above the din of the cars and trucks rumbling overhead on Route 94, even muting the noisy diesel horns. Looking straight at the man, still holding the bag, which contained some fruit and granola bars, "Man, when it is our time to leave, I command you to guard this bench. People may sit on it, but let no one defile it." The homeless man returned to his abode behind the big, blue tarp, munching on an apple.

For a moment, Jesse thought this was all an illusion, for he possessed a fertile imagination. The inner worlds of dreamtime, daytime flights of the imagination, mixed with the present reality of what was taking place before him on the macadam roadway informed his state of mind. They were the three primary tributaries that did not collide or conflict with each other but flowed together like the Big Black, Red and White rivers feeding into the nearby Mississippi, perfectly blending into the constant flow and rush of his life. He invited himself into this circumstance of Father John's funeral. He was fully aware of what was taking place but it disturbed him that Zach dignified the homeless man with spoken words but thoroughly ignored his attempts at conversation. He never experienced anything this strange. It was an otherworldly situation but he was impelled to persist to the very end in order to witness its unfolding.

Standing numb and helpless, he started to daydream in the face of an unwelcome situation, his mind boring through the walls of a past life, as if he cut the cord to reality. This is the real interior life, he thought, where the tributaries of his very existence were being spooled into an eddy, spinning out of control, becoming a multiplex cinema of unreality. Is he now inhabiting a parallel universe, prisoner of the dreamtime component only, the real world of *no* death and *no* taxes? The manner of the death of Father John might have been justified. He convinced himself he needed to to live with the results.

When Father John met Jesse and his girlfriend one day outside the supermarket, he did not know how to behave in their company. He reflected on the encounter and regretted not being gracious to her. He knew nothing about her, but immediately determined she was not right for Jesse, whom he adored. Jez was a purple rage rebel in her home. She smoked pot, drank excessively, cursed incessantly, slept around, told stories to her cousins who gathered round her whenever she showed up at family gatherings, captivated by her exotic tales which all proved to be true. Father John knew nothing of this but sensed a certain power within her.

Jesse was instantly attracted to Jez. He found out early in their relationship that she was highly intuitive. She possessed the ability to size up anyone within minutes of meeting them. Jesse watched in wonder as she primed the pump for all the information she needed to know about a person. The moment she realized that an individual was not authentic, she lost interest in going any further in pursuit of a relationship, even a casual one. If Father John had met a less imposing young woman that day with Jesse, he might have acted differently.

When Zach sat down, Jesse approached. He again made eye contact, making sure that Zach heard him and understood what he was saying. "When I got to the pool, there was no further mention of swimming without bathing trunks. That was a relief. I still think that was odd. I remember later on asking someone who would know if the Y had that policy and he said no. As you may or may not know, Father did not have an athletic physique. He was kind of built like a barrel. Not fat, just round with sparse hair on his chest. He wore a whistle around his neck, as if he were a swimming coach but he never did blow it." Jesse sensed that Zach wanted Jesse to return to his truck by the way he kept diverting his eyes to every vehicle coming over the rise. However, Jesse needed to tell him one more story while it was still fresh on his mind.

"There was another instance when I believe Father John acted strangely," he began, "I was in my second year of High School when we met outside the supermarket. He was coming out as we were going in ... *we* ... my girlfriend Jez and I."

This time, Zach focused intently when Jesse spoke. "I introduced Jez to Father and all of a sudden he is speaking, not to her, but to me in a voice I never heard before. It was shrill almost; words hopping out of his mouth at a rapid clip, varying from normal speaking voice to a falsetto high-pitch and then his voice would crack. I don't know how else to explain it. He rocked from side to side as he spoke, telling me silly things he did as a child, mixed in with telling me all the groceries he carried were for the poor. Then he stopped in the middle of a sentence and gave us a hurried goodbye. It was then that I noticed he wore open-toed sandals without socks. It was the middle of winter! The cuffs of his shirt and hems of his pants were frayed. He never once looked at Jez, but only for a quick glance as he rushed to his car. Jez asked me afterwards, Who was that? and What was that?"

Zach then located another speck of lint on his trousers, removed it, as the woman and girl resumed their grooming assignments.

Suddenly, the homeless man pulled aside the tarp and ran to the base of the ledge. He pointed to the road as he bellowed in a rapturous voice:

"Zachariah, look! I tell you
It is Elijah's chariot coming down the hill.
His body will rest between the cushioned rails
Lined with velvet as plush as the pillow
Upon which his head must lie.
The wide whitewall tires will be washed clean again
Before the sun-drenched trip to the heavens
And the winged angel upon the hood will hold
That victory wreath with outstretched arms
Charging up one hill and down the other.
The strips of gold that line the chassis vents
Will drive the engine to its ultimate power
As the seraphim and cherubim songs inside
Embrace his soul in the harmony of the universe."

Zach and the two females jumped up to meet the white stretch limousine as it pulled alongside the bench. The driver opened the door for the ladies, then sprayed each whitewall tire with a bubbly cleanser. The driver and Zach next opened the back gate and placed the casket and cart inside. Jesse did not get a good look at the interior but he expected to see either a pimp wearing a jelly roll hat passing champagne flutes to his hookers or a group of teenage prom girls and their dates swaying to raucous music.

The limo sped off. Jesse followed, trying to stay within fifty yards of the limo as it streaked along the winding river's bluff. As he drove, with much gratitude to the poet, Wallace Stevens, Jesse desired to know not the idea of the thing but the thing itself. He so yearned to delight in the 'new knowledge of reality', to dispose of the unreality that persisted in dominating his being, a person tossed into circumstances he never once controlled. He struggled to recall the moment when he turned away from feel and touch to think and conjure. In this very present, his hold on reality was tenuous. There was no one to talk to, only things and people and situations to talk about. As he drove, he reviewed the few conversations he had with Father John LeBarron. If he knew him better, there is more he could have said at the trial.

After his visit to the church courtyard in Atlantic City, John LeBarron never looked back. His passion for serving God by serving others simply blocked out all other needs and desires. He quit gambling and smoking immediately. He let go of his fondness for drink for long stretches, then periodically slipped back into that habit for equally long periods. That tormenting cycle repeated itself for the rest of his life. His bouts with sexual desire were just that, bouts, not the fullness of exploring his identity through the physical union with another human being. He was not sure who he was. Sexuality more confused him than tempted him. It was not as clear-cut and tangible as gambling, smoking and drinking. He strived to be perfect like his heavenly father is perfect but he was overly conscious of how far short he fell. His knowledge of his many failures and shortcomings depressed him greatly. No professor at seminary or colleague in the priesthood convinced him that he could actually be of great help to people despite his flawed, imperfect self.

***

Although they lived in the same city, Jesse and Father Johns' paths had not crossed in many years. But cross they did at Father John's trial. The following is the official transcript of the testimony given by Jesse Cairo at the trial of Father John LeBarron.

JESSE CAIRO, DEFENDANT'S WITNESS, SWORN

The Clerk: State your name and spell it for the record.
Witness: My name is Jesse Cairo, C-A-I-R-O.
The Court: Mr. Pointer, you may proceed.
Mr. Pointer: Thank you, Your Honor.
DIRECT EXAMINATION By Mr. Pointer
Q Good morning, Mr. Cairo.
A Good morning.
Q Do you know Mr. John LeBarron?
A Yes I do.
Q How long have you known Mr. LeBarron?
A Since I was in the eighth grade at St. Kilian's.
Q Have you ever attended the YMCA swimming pool in downtown St. Paul?
A Yes.
Q When?
A During the Christmas break in 1988.
Q Did anyone invite you to the pool?
A Yes.
Q Who?
A John LeBarron
Q Were you alone or with other people?
A With other people.
Q Who were the other people?
A Two other boys.

Q Anyone else?

A Well, Father John. I mean John LeBarron. He wasn't a priest yet.

Q Were you friends with the two other boys?

A I met them for the first time that day. They were in the pool when I got there.

Q What were their names?

A I don't know. John LeBarron never introduced us.

Q Can you describe them?

A How so?

Q Tell the court how old they were and what they looked like.

A They were about my age, I think. One boy was tall with dark hair. The other boy was short, kind of chubby, with curly red hair.

Q How old were you at the time?

A I was eleven.

Q How long were you at the pool?

A I think about an hour. John LeBarron told me that we would have the pool to ourselves for an hour.

Q You had the pool all to yourselves?

A Yes. Me, the two other boys and John LeBarron.

Q Were you wearing a bathing suit the entire hour?

A Yes.

Q What about the others?

A Everyone wore a suit.

Q Did the defendant touch you in anyway while you were at the pool?

A Yes.

Q Can you describe to the court how he touched you?

A He was standing in the four-foot area of the pool and asked me to come close to him.

Q Did you?

A Yes. I swam over to him.

Q Did he also ask the other boys to come to him?

A No. They stayed at the deep end, horsing around in the water.

Q What happened next?

A He took me by the shoulders and told me to cross my arms and use my left hand to support my right elbow, then pinch my nose with my right hand.

Q What did he say to you then?

A He told me to keep my mouth closed because he was going to dunk me and didn't want me to swallow water.

Q Did he handle you in an aggressive way?

A No. He grabbed me firmly but I didn't feel that he was being aggressive.

Q How did he grab you?

A He supported my back with his left arm and held his right hand across my hands when he dunked me.

Q Why did you let him do this?

A I thought it was a game.

Q Were you afraid?

A Not at all. I trusted him

Q How many times did he dunk you?

A Three times.

Q Did he say anything as he was dunking you?

A I could see his mouth moving when I was under water so I only heard a few words when I came up for air.

Q What words did you hear?

A Father. Son. Holy Spirit.

Q After swimming, did you shower and change in the locker room?

A No. John LeBarron said another group had the next

hour and we just had time to towel off and put our street clothes on.

Q How did you get home?

A John LeBarron drove us home in his car. He dropped me off first.

Q Where did you boys sit?

A We were all in the back seat.

Q Did you boys talk to each other?

A They played rock-paper-scissors the whole time.

Q Why didn't you play?

A It's just a hand game for two people.

The blinding late afternoon sun became a safety hazard for drivers, including Jesse. The road they travelled was a single lane in either direction. There were several blind turns that caused havoc when Jesse drove out of them, heading in a westerly direction, unprepared for the sudden burst of glaring sunlight coming in two streams through his windshield. He reached and grabbed his sunglasses out of the glove compartment, pulled down the peak of his baseball cap and dropped the sun visor each time he came out of a turn. He thought the limo driver was going too fast for the likes of this country road. Tractor-trailers whizzed by, heading in the opposite direction toward Rte. 94.

Jesse hit the pedal hard when he momentarily lost sight of the white chariot on one of the turns. This harrowing part of the drive lasted a full fifteen minutes before Jesse started to feel confident again that he had the limo within his sights. He was about seventy-five yards behind the limo, and needed to catch up. As he approached the next westerly turn on an uphill grade and was just about to pull the visor down, he could see a semi swerve over the dividing line and shear the side view mirror off the limo. Shaken, the limo driver jerked the steering wheel, trying to turn sharply away from the truck. The vehicle fishtailed. Trying to compensate and regain control, the driver braked hard, causing the back gate to pop open. The driver of the truck never knew his trailer hit anything and just kept rolling along.

What happened next seemed to take place in slow motion as Jesse could not believe the sick horror of what unfolded in front of him. The coffin, still on the cart, came flying out of the limo and separated when it made contact with the road. The coffin hit the ground hard and bounced several times on the pavement, with chips of wood filling the air with a spray of splinters. On the third bounce, John's corpse pitched out of the coffin and fell into a gully beyond the shoulder. In the next blink of an eye, Jesse saw the cart speeding toward him. He swerved to the right and stopped on the shoulder. He took several deep breaths and thought his pounding heart would explode out of his chest. He took another deep breath and saw Zach and the limo driver pick up the open casket, put it back into the vehicle, then drive off.

Did they not notice that the occupant of that casket was now lying in a ditch? Jesse had a decision to make, quickly. Catch up to them on this perilous road or recover the body. He made his decision. Driving slowly on the shoulder while looking to his right, he looked for the spot where he thought the body rolled into a ditch. He had made a mental note of the roadside sign that advertised the distance to several cemeteries. He knew with certainty that the body flew out of the coffin a few feet shy of that sign.

Jesse shut off the motor and sidled down the gully. For over an hour, the glaring sunlight beamed ahead of him every step he took, several particles of dust invaded his eyes and mouth, bent reeds smacked him in the face, and he had great difficulty navigating the uneven ground made hollow in places by voles digging holes. Despite the barriers, he trudged forward. The searing image of the man he once knew bounding and rolling on the asphalt assaulted his senses, yet he persisted, combing the area on foot, through thick, prickly brush, part of it marshy, his feet sinking into the moist earth every few steps as runoff water flowed between his unsteady legs through the culvert, toward the big river.

Exhausted, still shaken by what he just witnessed, he gathered himself and covered the same ground two more times with the same discouraging results.

He sat down on the water and picked the sticker burr weeds off his ankles, then realized he had lost one shoe in the marshy terrain. He was too tired to retrieve it and too emotionally spent to hunt down the limo, which now transported an empty coffin. The sun that caused so many near misses on the road that afternoon started its descent. Jesse returned to his pick-up and headed back to the transfer point.

When he arrived, the homeless man was waiting for him, standing next to the bench. "*Ecce homo,*" he said to the man.

"What does that mean?"

"If you know enough to call out Zachariah and Elijah, you know what those words mean."

The man looked at Jesse's feet and asked, "What happened to your other shoe?"

"It's a long story."

"Can I have that one?" he said, pointing to Jesse's right foot.

"What good is one shoe?"

"One is better than none."

Jesse looked down at the man's feet and saw the man's swollen, fungus-infected toes poking through crudely made footwear, cobbled together from truck tire shards he salvaged from the highway overhead.

"Can you tell me anything about the people in that family?"

"A little bit, maybe. Which one?"

"Zach?"

"He is very tall."

"And dresses nicely," Jesse said.

"I guess you're right about that."

"How about his wife?"

"That's not his wife," the man said in a manner suggesting he expected Jesse to know the answer to the question beforehand, "She's his sister."

"How about the little girl?"

"I know her best," the man said, his eyes tearing.

"How so?" Jesse inquired.

After a moment's hesitation, the man lowered his head and cried, "I was hungry and she gave me something to eat."

With that, Jesse lost his composure and wept. He hugged the man, embracing him closely, despite the homeless man's noxious odor and head-to-toe filth.

When the men broke their embrace, Jesse looked at the bench as if seeing it for the first time. It was hand crafted out of alternating horizontal planks of cedar and cypress. There was no metal on any part of the bench. It was supported underneath by thick olivewood planks that were cross-beamed on either end. All joints were held together with hand carved wood pegs. Gourds, palm trees and open flowers were delicately carved into each plank, outlined on the edges with gold paint.

There was just a little light left to the day as Jesse noticed that one of the cedar planks was bereft of any carved figures. He looked at the man and asked, "May I carve some good words into this plank?" pressing his palm down upon the intended spot.

"No you may not," the man said firmly, "This bench cannot be defiled".

"If I can guarantee you that it will be an improvement and not a defilement, will you trust me to do it?" There followed a moment of silence, indicating it was not worth considering rather than any actual consideration was even taking place, "You have no reason to trust me. That's why I'm giving you the keys to my truck," he said as he held out the keys, "And I'll walk home barefooted if you're not satisfied. Not only that. I'm a woodcarver, not by trade, but a pretty damn good amateur. It's too dark to carve now. I'll come back tomorrow with food, a pair of boots for you and I'll bring my tools along with can of gold paint."

"Before we waste any more of each other's time, tell me the words you want to carve," the man demanded.

Jesse retrieved a piece of notepaper out of his truck and wrote these words for the man to approve: '*The word of the Lord in your mouth is truth*'. The man nodded his approval and handed the truck keys back to Jesse.

"I told you I would walk home so you would trust me," Jesse said, seriously.

"Keep your truck. What would I do with it? I got everything I need up there," the man said as he pointed to his blue tarp home beneath the highway, "besides I don't think you'd last longer than two miles before you'd be pissing and moaning about your sore feet." The man turned and headed up to the incline.

He turned around and asked Jesse, "So, did they find the cemetery all right?"

"Father John is right where he always wanted to be," Jesse said, "I'll visit again tomorrow."

Acknowledgements

Acknowledgement and appreciation are due the following publications in which some of the short stories in this collection first appeared:

"Enlightenment At Big Bend" *The Almagre Review, Issue 4, Winter 2017-2018*

"Asylum, Asylum" *The Main Street Rag, Vol 23, Number 22*

"The Farm" *Palo Alto Review, Vol xxiv*

"Live Music Today" *Opossum, Fall 2018*

"The Baptism" *North Dakota Quarterly, Vol 85, Numbers 1-4*

THE AUTHOR

Jack Donahue is a poet, short story writer, novelist and playwright. Numerous poems and works of fiction written by Jack Donahue have been published in magazines and literary arts journals such as: *Takahe* (New Zealand); *Bindweed* (Ireland); *Stand* (U.K.); *Poetry Salzburg Review* (Austria); *Raconteur, The Main Street Rag; Armarolla* (Cyprus); *Opossum*; *North Dakota Quarterly*; *The Almagre Review* and many other journals and magazines throughout North America, Europe and Asia. Donahue's first novel *Lost on Cherry Street* was published by Willow River Press, MN. His second novel, *Divine Intimacy* was published by Guernica Editions, Gananoque, Canada. His second book of poetry, *Warning Signs* was published by Meat for Tea Press, MA. Jack Donahue received his BA in English from Long Island University, Brooklyn Campus, NY; and earned his Master of Divinity Degree from New Brunswick Theological Seminary, New Jersey. He is married to Carol Donahue, a children's picture book author. They reside in Centerport, NY.

www.ingramcontent.com/pod-product-compliance
Lightning Source LLC
Chambersburg PA
CBHW020153310726
48970CB00006B/2133